THE
STRAITS
OF
FLORIDA

MARTY COX

Dedicated to my cousin Mark Levee,
a gentle giant of a man

ACKNOWLEDGEMENTS

To Fran Cooper, who showed me how to turn paragraphs into pages. Sharon Smith, who did a magnificent job of editing and Estelle Wolf, who tied all the loose strings together. In addition, I'd like to thank to all the people that drifted into and out of my life to make this story possible.

STRAITS OF FLORIDA

The Strait carries the Florida Current, which is the beginning of the Gulf Stream from the Gulf of Mexico into the Atlantic Ocean, passing between the Florida Keys and Cuba. It is only 93 mi. (150 km.) wide at its narrowest point, between Key West and the Cuban shore, and in some areas plunges in depth to over 6,000 feet.

CHAPTER 1

1961

AFTER ACTION REPORT

Even though we are many, many miles south of Miami, the city's millions of lights were reflecting off low hanging clouds making the horizon look like day. Here in this mangrove swamp on a small island in the Florida Keys it is very dark, very hot and very humid. Every so often, a gator bumps the boat causing it to rock slightly for a short time only then to be bumped again by another gator. The air is filled with the high pitched, angry sound of mosquitoes seeking a place to land so they can suck on human blood. The wind is dead calm. The odor of dead vegetation and stagnant salt water hang so heavy in the air you could cut it with a knife. The smell of decay is as inescapable as are the insects. Waiting to get underway, waiting to move out of this cesspool is nerve racking and both literally and figuratively painful.

Our 50-foot boat is loaded with weapons and ammunition, everything checked, rechecked, and checked again. In two

1

minutes, at twenty two hundred hours, (10 p.m.) we will be on our way. Our destination, a small bay East of Havana, Cuba, 220 Degrees South, Southwest of Key West, a distance of 97 nautical miles.

The three of us, Jorge, Rafael, and me are below deck, crammed between the cargo and instrument panels. The charts of our target area are spread out over the ships wheel. To help with our night vision, we use the red lights from our flashlights to go over the course for the tenth time. This is not the first time we are making a trip like this but the first time we are operating as a team, and the first time we will be operating this close to Havana with the Cubans now having Russian equipment and aircraft.

Our objective is to make contact with anti-Castro forces and offload weapons and ammunition successfully without being involved in a firefight. Our instructions are clear.

Deliver our cargo, but under no circumstance return gunfire if any problems develop.

The operation and planning for a successful outcome of this mission has been done by a group sitting somewhere in Miami, with the input, intelligence, and blessings from Washington. On this venture, as in all others, we were just delivery boys.

The Cuban population of Miami is a tightly knit community, politically divided between Castro and Batista factions. However, politics aside, all were supporting each other, striving to be successful in their new land. All have experienced the common thread and the traumatic emotion of leaving Cuba, family, and friends behind. Those whom accumulated their assets under Batista, were prudently shifting their assets and relocating from Cuba to Miami. As Castro made more in-roads on the eastern end of Cuba, the larger the number and faster Batista supporters left. Anti-Castro Cubans, seeing how the new Cuba was emerging and fearing for the future, emigrated any way they could. Coming ashore by any means on the Florida Peninsula hopefully alive, with nothing more than the clothes on their backs and what, if they were fortunate, had smuggled out.

As in all times of forced migration, cash and jewelry were the easiest things to barter and the easiest to hide and sew inside clothing when relocating to another Country. It took only a short time after Fidel came into power to start this exodus. Those caught attempting to leave Cuba with any assets was instantly given the death penalty as the reward for trying.

Fortunately, Cuban banks, boutiques, businesses, and restaurants were already revitalizing a decade and a half of Miami's decay with the city gladly welcoming the newcomers. While the majority settled in, some had a fierce determination to return to Cuba and overthrow the Castro regime. My friends Jorge and Rafael were of this group.

My mind drifted back to last night. Jorge, Rafael and their wives joined me for dinner at one of our favorite Cuban restaurants in Little Havana. Our trip was no secret to them. Their wives knew where we were headed. Although the dinner was excellent, the talk was restrained and the atmosphere somber. After a few hours, and more than a few drinks, the small talk fizzled out. They left for home and I caught a taxi to my hotel. I do not believe anyone slept that night, in anticipation of the coming day.

In the few moments before the engines were turned on, I looked at my two shipmates. Jorge, I have known for nearly a decade and I smiled thinking how we met by chance at a Cuban Air Force base in Havana where destiny made us as close as brothers and whose sister I was going to marry. Rafael, the third member of our triumvirate, as close as a friend could be, who came to Cuba from Spain as a child and whose family now reside in Miami. Both moves made necessary for voicing their opinion against dictatorships, Franco from Spain and Castro from Cuba. However, last night was the second time I had had the opportunity to meet their wives; warm, intelligent, educated women, who for the next few days will be under tremendous strain. I hope that having small babies to take care of will give them something to concentrate on rather than the risk their husbands are taking.

We cast off our lines as slowly, as quietly as possible, started our muffled engines, and begin working our way out of the lagoon, then into the bay. Our heading takes us in a southerly direction between the islands making our way to the last of the Florida Keys and into the North flowing Gulf Stream. Our navigation lights are on to conform to Coast Guard regulations, but as soon as we clear Key West, they will be turned off. As for the radios, we disconnected them to insure they would not be turned on inadvertently to allow Cuban direction finders to pick up our radio waves. Under the soles of our feet, we could feel the suppressed power of the engines by the slight vibration of the deck as the propeller cuts into the water. My hope is that in this lagoon no roots or debris will wrap around our propeller shaft or dent the propeller blades. If that happened, at high speeds the vibration of propellers out of sync would tear the boat apart in a very short time. Via con dios! (Go with God). We are running dark and silent.

The moon would not show its face tonight or for several more nights, but the stars, as they say, were twinkling in all their glory. I prayed the weatherman called it right and soon, we would be under heavy cloud cover and rain. In this type of operation, bad weather is the perfect weather and the only weather for what we are about to attempt.

There is no idol conversation once an operation such as this is under way. Everyone becomes focused on what needs to be done, anticipating, and planning for anything that may come up. I was no different but for some reason this was the first time I had ambivalent feelings about the positive outcome of this trip. I again glanced at my friends and thought " how ironic" for the fates to conspire over years to put us together on this boat tonight doing what we were going to do and the reasons for doing it. Jorge, to get back at Castro for the prestige, wealth and position Castro ripped from his family. Rafael, for the sake of adventure and his radio talk show, and me for what I left in Cuba, a future wife and a baby son I may never see.

For the hundredth time, I went over every aspect of this voyage. Is the cargo tied down and secure in the event of heavy seas? Do we have enough fuel? Are the compasses corrected? Are the charts up to date? What small detail have I overlooked? What if?

What if? Well it is all in the past. We were moving. We were committed. The key is to survive "in the now."

Four hours later, we are inside Cuban territorial waters. The stars were covered by clouds and we have already passed through a few heavy rainsqualls. Raindrops felt great on our skin and tasted delicious when we raised our faces, open our mouths, and let the cool water that has fallen hundreds of feet trickle down our throats. I always found that fear and anticipation always made my mouth dry and this trip is no exception.

The sea picked up a bit, but fortunately, the ceiling is lowering and heavy rains were moving in fast. Tropical rain combined with wind driven spray made it more difficult for radar to pick us up. However, in life, everything seems to balance. With rain and cloud cover on one hand, it was balanced by lightning flashes on the other, which could give away our position. Life is a gamble, so I thought, "Thank the Gods for little favors."

We made landfall, right on target. A flashlight was blinking at us from shore that was easy to spot even through the heavy rain. Our contacts were there as planned. We trained in on the light source, cut our engines, and slowly drifted between cliffs on either side of us, into a small bay. We quietly released the anchor and anxiously awaited the rowboats coming out to offload our cargo. The tide slowly swung our stern to the beach pointing our bow to the open sea. It is quiet. The boat is slowly rising and falling with the long swells before they crest on the bar to become small surf. The tropical foliage smells sweet. Combined with the rain and salt in the air, the scent is so heavy you can taste it. For a moment, with the slight undulations of the boat as it pulls on the anchor line, all thoughts drift out of my mind and I am completely out of reality, in perfect harmony with life, the sea, and nature. Then it happened! In the rain, a red speck of light lifts from the ocean into the low hanging clouds.

About a quarter of a mile off our starboard bow, a siren blasts, a star shell explodes overhead turning the entire area into day and a parachute flare slowly descends. Immediately our boat was caught in the beam of a searchlight. In this small bay with the military on the beach shooting at us, cliffs confining us on both sides, and a Cuban patrol boat racing towards us from the ocean. We are boxed in!

Fortunately, all the guns and ammunition are on the stern deck ready to be offloaded. Working quickly as a team, the anchor line is cut, the cargo dumped over the side and the engines advanced to full throttle. We speed out of the bay, leaving us broadside and vulnerable to enemy fire. Without cargo, we are at least 40 knots faster than the Cuban patrol boat and in a few minutes, out of range of all her hand held guns. Our only concern is the 20mm canon on their foredeck. Thankfully, while being exposed like this, for whatever reason, the patrol boat doesn't take advantage of the situation and open fire. To surrender or be captured is out of the question. We know the outcome of that scenario very well, not only for us but also for Jorge's family who are still in Cuba.

Without weapons the safest maneuver is to head directly toward the incoming Cuban craft giving them the smallest target and making them hesitate before taking any action. Playing chicken, going head to head, taking the offensive whether between aircraft, cars, or boats is the only action to take when cornered in someone else's backyard. It is the only way to have a chance for survival.

The designer of our boat was someone I knew from the Jersey Coast. He was constructing them for the Navy in New Jersey as well as building them for the DEA in Miami. The boat had the design and power needed when being chased by 2,000 ft. per second cannon shells or 1200 ft. /sec, 9-millimeter automatic rifle bullets. With 1,000 horsepower engines driving twin screws, going over 60 knots in calm or heavy seas, you are a very difficult target skipping over wave tops especially at night. We headed directly towards the Cuban patrol boat, directly into harm's way.

The three of us were in the cockpit, hiding behind the windscreen protected from the rain. At the speed we are moving, raindrops hitting us would feel like bullets. Our kidney belts, as well as our seat belts, are pulled as tight as they could be to prevent our kidneys jarring loose and keep us from being bounced overboard. Survival was our primary thought.

The parachute flare hit the water; it was dark again but the patrol boat's searchlight held us in its beam as we closed the distance. Now only about 200 yards bow to bow. They finally opened up with automatic weapons, but with the closing speed and choppy seas, tracers were passing well over our boat. Yet instinctively, we still ducked from the muzzle flashes.

My mind raced to find a game plan. Should I ram the side of their boat hoping to hole it and on passing, be at the mercy of their automatic weapons? Or, getting close should I turn the wheel hard to starboard, spray them with a huge wash, blinding them for a few seconds then running due North to International waters, while still being a target for their cannon?

In either case, now that we were being tracked, the key to survival was getting into International waters as fast as possible and hopefully, the U.S. Coast Guard or Navy will have a ship, fully armed waiting for us. This will be the longest 12 miles in our lives.

Then, from somewhere deep in my memory came a bit of sea lore. In ancient times before ships had rudders on their centerline, boats were steered by use of a specialized oar held by a sailor located at the stern of the boat. However, like most of society, there was many more right- handed sailors than left- handed. This meant that the right-handed sailors holding the steering oar (which had been broadened to provide better control) used to stand on the right side of the boat. For that reason, by custom, most of today's small boats have their steering wheel on the right side of the craft.

If another boat is coming at you head on, it's instinctive to turn to the right to put the port side of your craft, the side furthest from you, to bear the brunt of a collision, a brilliant strategy IF their steering is on the starboard side of their boat and IF the Cuban quartermaster reacts normally. I put the plan into motion.

From their perspective, it must have been a frightening sight-seeing the bow of a boat 50 feet in length roaring directly at them, seemingly right up the narrow beam of their searchlight with a combined closing speed of over 80 knots. Then a tremendous flash of lightning illuminated the scene as I swung the wheel to starboard. The Cuban boat turned to the right, as I hoped it would. Our high-speed turn, threw a wall of water well over their deck and pilothouse. Unfortunately, one of the Cuban sailors was thrown from the deck of their patrol boat directly into our path. He must have been cut in two when he hit our bow and then chewed up by the propellers.

It worked! Our stern was now facing the patrol boat making us a very difficult target. We are doing over 60 knots and leaving "Dodge" fast heading north.

The three of us breathed a collective sigh of relief. Looking at my watch, I was amazed; the entire episode took less than five minutes, but the intensity of those five minutes did not seem to fully register in our minds or emotions. We were numb.

Other than losing our cargo, we are in good shape, and hopefully with the weather as it was and the ceiling as low, the chances that a Cuban aircraft would be sent out to find us was minimal.

Then, as if reading my mind, an avenging Cuban angel, a MIG dropped through the clouds on our port beam making a pass with its landing lights on. Fortunately for us with all the electric storms in the area, breaking seas, spray, combined with salt in the air we hoped the plane's radar would operate no better than the radar on the patrol boat.

Spotted by the pilot during one of the lightning flashes also seemed to be no problem.

Lightening will greatly diminish a pilot's night vision and with this low ceiling, the low altitude and minimum speed he is flying, he could not afford to keep his eyes out of the cockpit for any extended periods of time, other than for an occasional glimpse. His fear, especially in a low speed turn, would be to inadvertently dip a wing into the sea. Our problem was being seen by the patrol boat. With the lightning flashes, they could radio our position to the pilot easily vectoring him in on us. If that happened, with their positioning report, coupled with the plane's landing lights, the guns on the MIG, and still being in Cuban waters, we're dead!

Reaching International waters was now out of the question. We had only one hope to survive. Slow the boat down and tie a line to the throttles. When we jumped overboard, we would pull the line and reset the boat to full throttle. Hopefully, the Cubans would follow the boat and destroy it. Later in the day when we could, we would turn on the homing beacons on our life jackets and be picked up by some U.S. ship. To me there was no other choice and no time to debate our options.

I explained my plan to Jorge and Raphael but they are reluctant to do it. They felt more comfortable staying with the craft at speed rather than rolling off a moving boat into the Florida Straits, an option that we never thought about, much less ever saw or tried in training.

There comes a time, when every man has to make a choice on how to survive. There is no right or wrong. There is no flipping a coin. There is only one outcome to your individual decision no matter what you factor in. There is no voting on the rest of your life. There is no time for a round table discussion. Your choice and decision is immediate. Your result—seeing tomorrow's sunrise or eternity. Jorge and Rafael's decision was to stay with the boat, my choice, the ocean.

Even with the engines slowed, the cockpit was too narrow, too noisy, and vibrating too much to do anything but form the words " good luck" and shake hands with Jorge and Rafael. I climbed to the deck and cautiously and slowly moved aft to the stern. Thunder and lightning still hovered above but fortunately, the rain was so heavy it pounded the seas down to moderate swells. Between lightning flashes, the ocean remained a black void showing only a dim white wake extending south from the boat's stern. I jumped and immediately heard the boat go to full throttle heading north to safety ten long minutes away.

Hitting the water felt as if I smashed into a brick wall. I tried to pull the tabs to inflate the life jacket but realized both my shoulders were dislocated from the impact. Fortunately, the tabs were close to my mouth so I used my teeth to pull the tabs and the jacket inflated. With my head resting against the back of the life jacket, cold to the core, in pain, my nerves on edge, I attempted to get my thoughts collected. Then, in what seemed a matter of seconds, the landing lights of the MIG passed so low over me, I was encapsulated in a bubble of intense sound as it tracked the wake of the departing boat. There was a short burst of cannon fire and the boat exploded. My immediate thought was, "Did my two friends survive the blast"?

The thought of rescue, for my comrades or me, if they were still alive, was a distant hope as I drifted for an indeterminate length of time. My body finally shut down due to hypothermia and I slowly lost consciousness. My last thoughts were, if I survive, how to explain the deaths of Jorge and Rafael to their wives if in fact that is what happened.

When I opened my eyes, the sun was well above the horizon. I heard voices and turned my head towards the sound and saw a small Zodiac being rowed towards me. Behind the Zodiac, a surfaced submarine with American markings. The homing device must have been triggered with my impact of hitting the water. I have no recollection of turning it on.

They transported me back to the Key West submarine base where surgery was performed to relocate my shoulders and given medication to control the pain. My stay in the Base hospital was only for a few days after which I was cleared medically, debriefed by the people I was affiliated with, and was asked to complete an "After Action Report". There was one more duty I had to perform. The bodies of Jorge and Rafael were found floating near the wrecked boat by the Navy and my last duty was to get back to Miami and explain to their wives what happened.

END OF AFTER ACTION REPORT

One of the Navy Corpsmen, I made friends with, offered to drive me to Miami, an offer I graciously refused. It was easier to rent a car, not be engaged in small talk for a few hours, and concentrate on how I was going to approach the subject. The subject and meetings I dreaded.

My first telephone call was to Jorge's wife. The phone rang at least ten times with no answer. I drove to the apartment and knocked on the door. This was also fruitless and when I was about to leave, the door of a nearby apartment opened and an elderly woman appeared, "Who are you looking for?"

"Mrs. Rodriguez," I replied." "I'm a very old and close friend of her husband Jorge, it's very important I speak to her."

She looked at me closely as if turning over in her mind what to do.

"Gloria is staying at her Mother's house on Key Biscayne. She just had a baby boy a few days ago and is resting there."

"Do you have the address? I would be very grateful if you gave it to me."

She went back into her apartment and a few minutes later came out with the address on a piece of paper and handed it to me.

"Tell her that Roberta says hello and wishes her and the baby, all the luck in the world, and that I'm making a blanket for the baby."

With that, she said goodbye and closed the door. Clutching the address, I walked back to the car and opened a street map of Miami and Key Biscayne.

Driving to Key Biscayne was extremely stressful. I found myself driving well under the speed limit, prolonging the encounter, as much as possible, but eventually arrived at my destination. It was a well-cared for cottage with attractive flowerbeds, surrounded by a manicured lawn. Reluctantly, I got out of the car and walked to the front door. As soon as I raised my hand to knock on the door, a trim gentleman in his early sixties opened it. I assumed the elderly woman who gave me the address must have called ahead.

"I'm."

"I know who you are."

"Can I please speak to Gloria?"

"I don't think now is the time", he said.

Then from inside the house a woman's voice called, "Carlos, where are your manners? Don please come in".

With anger turning his checks red, he opened the door wider so I could pass him as I went into the house. There in a wheelchair, sat an attractive woman whom I found out later was his wife Rosa, Gloria's mother.

"An hour ago we received a call from someone in Key West telling us about what happened to Jorge and that you were coming to see Gloria. Please sit down, we were expecting you."

Carlos, please relax and serve our guest a drink. Would you prefer rum, coffee?"

"No thanks. I need to explain everything to Gloria. Is she here?"

Then I heard a shout from another room.

"Leave here. You killed my baby's father and my husband. I never want to see or hear from you again."

Carlos got up from his chair.

"You heard my daughter; we would appreciate your leaving now."

"Can I explain what happened?" I asked looking at both of them.

"You heard my daughter- gringo leave!" Carlos pointed to the door.

I left!

Sitting in the car, composing myself, I went over my unwanted visit, realizing what an impact our actions had on so many people. I checked the address and map for Rafael's home, and put the car into gear. Half way there, I stopped for coffee in Little Havana, needing time to think about what I was going to say, but still too upset to call ahead for fear of the same reaction I got from Jorge's wife.

Rafael was the one member of our group whose family who was financially well off, and it was very apparent with the luxurious twenty story building they lived in, looking over Biscayne Bay in Coconut Grove. I walked into the lobby and was instantly stopped by a security guard.

"Who you looking for?"

"Carla Nunez or the apartment of Rafael Nunez."

"Are they expecting you?"

"No, but tell her Don, an old friend from Cuba is here to speak to speak to her."

He lifted the phone, dialed a number, which was answered instantly. I recognized the voice of Carla on the other end. The guard repeated what I had told him to say. Then he pressed the phone closer to his ear so that I could not hear. All I heard was, yes, yes, yes. He hung up looked at me and said, "She said she doesn't want to ever see you, leave immediately and I should call the police if you ever come here again. She also said you gave her enough bad luck to last a lifetime".

It's over! I'm devastated! I lost friends, my Cuban family, my honor, my pride.

My only consolation was taking a room at the DuPont, sitting by the window looking at the boats tied to the pier, cradling a bottle of scotch, drinking myself into short- term oblivion, going over it repeatedly, how it all began.

On a side street off Calle Ocho in the Little Havana section of Miami, there's a small park, where under the shade trees, "Los Viejos" the old Cuban men gather to sip their cafe cubanos, reminisce about Cuba and play dominoes.

If you look close there's also a small monument dedicated to people that gave up their new life and safety of being in the United States, to bring the fight back to free Cuba.

When I am down that way, after a few mojitos, my last glass is always raised to my brother Jorge, my dear friend Rafael, a wife I will never have and a son I will never hold.

Chapter 2

EAST HARBOR, MAINE

*E*ast Harbor is one of the many quaint fishing villages along the coast
of Maine where people of any age or lifestyle would be fortunate to find. A
year round community that offers the peace and tranquility of small town
living plus the advantage for many to express their creativity while enjoying the varied moods of the Atlantic. One benefit for me, a class in writing
at the local Community College. Most of the people in my writing class
were retired with the majority writing their memoirs for future generations.
Others were writing children's books, and a few authors, novels that the
public is unknowingly waiting to read, when and if the authors complete
or publish their works.

For over a year I sat alongside a man, a little older than myself, whom
to me seemed an enigma. He was of average height, graying hair, friendly
but reserved. When he spoke his light blue eyes never wavered from looking
directly at you. I never saw him angry or upset, no matter the occasion but
you could sense the strength behind his placid exterior. When he walked, it
was with the assistance of a walker and with every step, his facial expressions reflected the pain it was causing.

Each week he would read to the group something humorous, about another part of the world, or an adventure that may or may not have happened to him. None of these stories was ever in the "first person" and when asked, he would only smile, shrug his shoulders and change the subject.

After class, we would all gather at a local restaurant for lunch and as people do over time, try to sit alongside someone you seem to be most compatible with. That is what happened with Don and me. After many lunches and getting to know each other, we broke away from the class and at least once a week, started to meet for lunch, dinner, or coffee by ourselves.

With trust, my friend's inner person started unwrapping one layer at a time like the dough in a croissant. One fall evening, while having dinner, with autumn leaves falling, wind rattling the windows of the restaurant and the fireplace flickering, he opened his briefcase and took out a few handwritten pages and a diary.

"I started this story a while ago," he said. "I am no writer and I never shared this or my diary with anyone. I'm moving on in years, tired, constantly in pain and would like to tell somebody the full story before I die. As my friend, would you please take the time to read the few pages I wrote and the diary I kept and help me turn it into a book."

I looked at his face, really looked at his face for the first time. Not only did I see the agony he was in physically but also the pain of loneliness. The lines on his face from exposure to the elements, the deep wrinkles at the corners of his eyes all made me realize that the stories he wrote about the sea, the travels, and relationships were about him.

"What I'm concerned about is getting all the feelings I have had bottled up for so long to come out, so I can get a night's sleep without dreaming of what happened years ago, over and over and over again. That is my prime purpose. If someone can learn a lesson from my experience, so be it. Release is my prime objective. Release is what I'm looking for."

"Don, I'm no author and I'm sure I couldn't do justice to what you wrote, but I would sincerely enjoy listening to your story. Would you mind if I taped it?"

He looked out the window alongside our table that was facing the small bay. In a few weeks, the surface would be frozen over. I remember that night as if it were yesterday. The pole lights on the pier, strung on wires, were swaying wildly in the wind. Each lamp casting its' intermit-

tent yellow light on the small lobster boats tied alongside and then on the water lapping at the pilings. Through the thin windowpanes, we could hear the small boats straining against their wharf lines, each boat creaking and groaning trying to be set free. The clanging sound as the wind whipped the loose rigging against the aluminum masts of sailboats in the water since summer. A marine symphony accompanied by a chorus of hungry seagulls and the low moan of a distant foghorn. The night, the sounds, the crackling and popping of the fireplace of this old, weatherbeaten restaurant gave a feeling of warmth and security that was the perfect setting to bare one's soul.

Don's gaze returned from the outside to me. At that instant, I think we both had the feeling of being kindred souls. He smiled, refilled his cup of coffee. His face softened, his eyes became moist as he handed me the papers.

"Please," he said.

I took them from his hand, nodded my head yes, and started to read into my recorder.

STRAITS OF FLORIDA

When I completed the first chapter I was in another time and place, took a deep breath, raised my head and realized Don was watching for my reaction to what I just read. His first few chapters showed me how impossible it was to have insight into another person's life experiences no matter how long or well you may think you know someone. Never in the wildest stretches of my imagination would I associate my friend with what I just read.

CHAPTER 3

DON'S STORY

Guantanamo, Cuba 1955

I was mentally kicking myself for being lazy and stupid. After all my years flying in the Navy, this was the first time I hadn't personally checked the plane overbefore signing the yellow "sign-off" sheet and was now paying for it. Watching the fuel gauge, going rapidly down on the instrument panel, could only mean that someone in the ground crew did not screw the fuel filler cap on tight enough and gas was being sucked out by the flow of air over the wing.

This was a scheduled trip to accumulate additional required flight hours. The flight plan was from Guantanamo to Havana and return. It was a great way to be away from the base and it's restrictions but a round trip flight of only a few hundred miles would help keep my skills up. As for the loss of fuel, sitting in the cockpit at 5,000 feet, I couldn't do anything but land as soon as possible.

Not pushing my luck, Batista Airfield was off my port quarter and never being this close to Havana before, my thought drifted to staying overnight at the airfield's Bachelor Officers Quarters at Batista, and taking a short taxi ride to enjoy Havana's nightlife. A win, win situation. The very least would be that in the event I didn't get into Havana, the food and the bed would be a different experience here. I radioed the Batista control tower requesting permission to land.

"Batista tower: U.S. Navy 624 requesting immediate clearance to land."

"Navy 624 declare your emergency."

"Batista Tower, Navy 624 low on fuel."

"Navy 614 Affirmative, cleared to land straight in, runway 27, winds calm, altimeter 29.30."

"Batista Tower, Navy 624. Cleared to land, runway 27, winds calm, Altimeter 29.30."

I repeated the instructions back to the tower, cut the throttle, lowered the landing gear, extended the flaps and made my approach, landing without incident.

The "Follow Me" truck led me to the "Visitors Tie Down." I turned the engineoff, locked the brakes and controls, climbed down, and checked the fuel caps. Sure enough one cap was hanging from its chain. A learning experience I promised never to be repeated with the immediate thought of how the loss of fuel could have turned into a nightmare, or from what I heard, a night of unbridled revelry in Havana.

I asked the truck driver about getting something to eat so he dropped me off at a building I thought was the Bachelor Officer's Quarters (BOQ). I walked to the entrance, opened two magnificent wooden doors, and stopped in stunned silence looking into an exquisite formal dining hall. It was a setting out of a Hollywood movie; linen tablecloths on every table, candle light reflecting off crystal and silverware settings. Waiters, all in red vests, stood at "parade rest" against the rear wall. The entire dining area was bathed in dim lights, while live musicians were playing a slow rumba. With not a uniform in sight, the men were all dressed conservatively in suits, white shirts, and ties. The women in fashionable dresses. The one exception was a Major, in uniform, who approached me with a decided look of distaste on his face. Staring at me in flight gear like something the cat dragged in, he beckoned me away from the entrance then escorted me a few paces to where a Corporal was seated behind a partition.

"Lieutenant Commander, why are you here and in flight gear?" the Major asked. I explained my aborted flight due to fuel problems and the need to make an immediate landing and that it was the driver who dropped me off here after I requested to be taken to get something to eat. After inspecting me again, more slowly this time from my shoes to my sunglasses as if I were a specimen under a microscope, he said, "You can stay the night but you cannot come into the club dressed in flight gear.

We do have a room available for you to stay the night and dinner is served in the Officers Mess until 9 p.m., Corporal, give me a key."

He took the key from the enlisted man, gave it to me, holding it between thumb and forefinger, as if it was germ laden. "Please leave immediately," he said as he pointed to the door, "Ask someone outside where BOQ is," and with emphasis stressed, "This isn't it!"

Opening the door to my assigned room, I found a young man about my age laying on one of the beds, in pants, no shirt, no shoes, looking totally relaxed and comfortable, reading a book. We looked at each other; I motioned to the other bed and in Spanish said, "I guess they had no single rooms, do you mind my bunking here for the night?"

"Hell no gringo," my new roommate responded in English. He stood up put out his hand and said all in one breath, "You saved me from a dull evening. My name is Jorge. Have you plans for this evening? I'm bored, how about going to Havana with me. It will be a personally guided tour of the dens of inequity, bars, nightclubs, and casinos by one Captain Jorge Rodriguez of the Cuban Air Force. But first, do you have the time, money and stamina for it, money being most important", as he put out his hand to shake mine, "since the Cuban Air Force doesn't get paid until next Tuesday".

With his sense of humor and offer, we shook hands, I said yes to all, adding, "My name is Don".

How lucky can a guy be? An escorted tour of Havana with someone who knows the area. Being about the same size, Jorge loaned me a pair of his slacks and a Guayabara shirt. Even though I have been based in Guantanamo for over a year, this was my first opportunity to visit Havana and knew Jorge would turn out to be the perfect host and guide. Not only did he know the places I wanted to see or had heard about but would take me to places where the locals, not tourists congregate.

We started at the Tropicana with its fabulous chorus line of scantily clad women.

Then onto the sophisticated Hotel Nacional where it seemed half the patrons were American tourist and the other half the cream of Cuban society. Tuxedos and evening gowns were the prevailing dress code here. The next few places included Sloppy Joes and Hemingway's hangout. I don't recall how many places we visited after that. Each one had its' own tempo, but the one that made the most impression, representing the real Cuba, was "El Tempesto" in the slums of Havana. A strictly Cuban working class nightclub where everyone moved to an Afro-Cuban beat, where cigar smoke hung like a low hanging cloud, where dungarees and half-dressed women were the norm and liquor was sold by the bottle not the glass. Wherever we stopped, Jorge was either known or greeted like a lost friend or longtime customer.

"This is great."

He smiled back and said, "Amigo, I hope you're enjoying yourself."

As the night drew on, I felt Jorge was not enjoying this as much as I was so I came right out and asked him.

"Jorge, you're getting more and more quiet, que paso?"

"Don, my friend, have you noticed anything?"

"Yes, I'm running out of money."

"Well my friend, as your guide, and never before having the pleasure of showing Havana to an American officer and gentleman, what did you expect?

Ask anyone, Rodriguez is expensive. Have you noticed anything else companiero."

"No," the liquor is great, the women are friendly, the music is fantastic, and the guide, though expensive, knows his way around Havana. What should I have noticed?"

"Don, mi amigo, all that glitters isn't gold, so states an English proverb."

"Every place we have been, every bar, the Nacional, Sloppy Joes, even, here in the slums, either are owned by the Americanos or pay tribute to your mafia. Cuba, through Batista, is owned and controlled by the American Government, Corporate America, and the American Mafia. We might as well be your protectorate like Puerto Rico and give up our identity. Our slums, low income, gambling, prostitutes, drug problem, and taxes have all been forced on us by your Country."

"Come on Jorge, relax."

"I can't my friend. Let me give you a bit of Cuban history. In 1952, Batista again seized power in Cuba in a coup against the elected President Prio Socorras. Three months before the upcoming elections, Batista knew he was sure to lose. Also running in this election but for a different office was a young attorney named Fidel Castro. Batista voided the results of the elections and declared himself the Prime Minister of Cuba and the head of the Armed Forces. Political groups throughout Cuba rejected the coup but none more vehemently then the students of the University of Havana. Just over a year after Batista's coup, a small group of revolutionaries led by Castro attacked the Moncada Army Barracks of Santiago de Cuba. The attack failed and Batista sent a note to the military commander ordering him to "kill ten rebels for every soldier killed" in the attack. "With Castro, our economy and Cuba, hopefully, once again will be controlled by Cubans. One last thing, last year in 1954, due to popular unrest, and to appease his U.S. friends, Batista held a mock election in which he was the only candidate. He naturally won becoming President of Cuba. He was so confident of his power that in 1955, this year, he released Castro from jail, with some of the remaining survivors of the Moncada attack, hoping to dissuade some of his critics. Within weeks though, it was rumored that Batista's military police was looking to kill Castro, so the rebels went to Mexico to plan a new revolution. It's no secret that Fidel, who was then in Mexico, would return and anyone that's a true Cuban is looking forward to ousting Batista and all he represents, including your American mafia.

"Jorge, with all the rum I had, I cannot digest much of what you are saying, so since you lost the festive mood, and its late let me thank you for tonight and head back to the base. I have to be sober in the morning to fly back to Guantanamo.

With this serious note dampening our festivities as well as my depletion of funds, we took a taxi back to Batista as dawn was breaking in the eastern sky. We wobbled to our room and that's all I remembered until noon. That night started a friendship that eventually made us as close as brothers.

We got up about the same time, looked at each other, and jointly agreed on a scale of one to ten, we both looked and felt like a three. After showering, I dressed into my flight gear, Jorge in slacks and a polo shirt, and we walked out to the veranda where lunch was being served. Nearly everyone was in formal uniform, but again I stood out like a sore thumb, the "gringo" in flight gear and was guided to our own table for two.

"Jorge, where are all the pilots?"

"Every one sitting here is a pilot. The base is on stand down and there is no formal schedule at this time. Due to Castro's possible landing on the east end of Cuba, some of the pilots are waiting to be transported by truck, to a base closer to the action".

I avoided any further discussion that needed concentration and enjoyed a thoroughly delicious lunch. We both agreed that now we felt our scale of sobriety moved from three to six. He walked me out to my plane. I took the oxygen mask from my helmet, took a few deep breaths to help clear my head, and handed it to Jorge. In a few moments, we both reached a semblance of clear headedness. After ensuring the plane had been serviced and refueled, I doubled checked the gas caps and signed off the equivalent of the American yellow sheet.

Before I climbed into the cockpit, we shook hands, then in the Cuban way, put our arms around each other's shoulders, in an "Embrazo" and knew we would keep in touch.

"Gringo, let's make plans to meet somewhere next weekend. I'll show you other parts of Cuba and you tell me about the States."

"Rodriguez, I'd like that. In fact, I will call you Thursday night at the number you gave me, and if we're both free, it's a date. I'll bring the money, as it seems that commodity is always in short supply with you, and you bring the Chiquita's, agreed?"

With that, I climbed in, started the engine, got clearance from the tower, and took off. Flying back with a blue sky, a slight tail wind, fleecy white clouds, and sunshine, I had plenty of time to let my thoughts drift. What Jorge said started to play back in my mind, but economics and politics were something I knew or cared very little about. I never have been interested in delving into these subjects, much less International politics but there was something Jorge said that aroused my curiosity.

Here I am in Cuba with a Cuban President backed by American industry and Mafia on one hand, and Castro's revolutionary army who may be on it's way to the eastern end of the Island, on the other. I was in the middle of history and did not know anything about it. According to Jorge, Cuba was not all fun and games. In reflection, there seemed to be an underlying tension everywhere we went. I needed to expand my knowledge of what was happening.

I landed at Guantanamo with plenty of fuel; spent ten minutes giving the line chief hell about the loose gas cap, and couldn't wait to complete my daily tasks so I could get to the base library. Once there, I located a space away from everyone, collected as many American newspapers and magazines as I could relating to Cuba, and began to read.

I could not believe it. I've been sitting on a powder keg for nearly a year, never knowing or interested in what was happening around me.

It was reported that Batista murdered 20,000 people turning Cuba into a police state in his last coup to take over the Cuban

Government. I vaguely remembered reading in the newspapers that in the late 1940's, at the Waldorf Astoria Hotel in New York, Batista not only established a lasting business relationship with organized crime, but a renowned friendship with the American mobsters Meyer Lansky and Lucky Luciano, where under their rule Havana became known as the "Latin Las Vegas". It was at that meeting they agreed that in exchange for kickbacks to Batista, Lansky and the Mafia would control all the casinos and racetracks in Havana.

None of this was secret, nor was it a secret that in 1955 Batista was encouraging large scale gambling in Havana to anyone who invested one million American dollars in a hotel or 250,000 American dollars in a nightclub, the Cuban Government would provide matching public funds, a ten-year tax exemption and duty free importation of supplies, equipment and furnishings. His policy also waived background checks and opened the door for casino investors with illegally obtained sources of funding. It was no secret that besides the $250,000 to be paid to get a license, there was more often than not, an additional fee, sometimes more than the actual license fee required, that was paid under the table, going into Batista's bank account.

Apparently, Batista had every American Corporation in Cuba in his pocket.

ITT gave him a solid gold telephone as an expression of their gratitude for the excessive telephone rate increase. One oil company was given access to develop fifteen million acres to explore for oil, making it one of the five most traded stocks on the New York Exchange.

It was also well known that for a price, Batista handed out contracts for highway and airport construction to favored American companies, as well as power companies, train lines and even a strange plan to build a canal across Cuba.

Meanwhile the average family had an income of $6 a week with only a third of the homes having running water. To add to the discontent, Cuba had a twenty percent unemployment rate. Arthur M. Schlesinger documented all of this when the United States Government asked him to analyze Batista's Cuba.

With the corruption of the government, the brutality of the police, the regime's indifference to the needs of the people for education, medical care, housing, social justice and economic justice I could easily see an invitation for a change of government and the festering dislike of all "gringos".

CHAPTER 4

I was looking forward to the possibility of seeing Jorge next week. He was sharp-minded, cultured and seemed to know many interesting people. If nothing else, it would improve my Spanish, as well as, my knowledge of the culture and politics of Cuba. I owed him for showing me a great time in Havana, and for opening my eyes as to what was actually happening around me. I called on Thursday and we made plans to meet that weekend, halfway between Havana and Guantanamo. I took the train and he drove.

The train ride was quite an experience. The train itself, which must have been built in the early 1900's, had no individual seats; seating was mere benches down both sides of the cars. Between the benches was a wide aisle ample enough for people to move about, store their crates of chicken, goats, and produce, while dogs roamed freely. Window frames contained no glass, allowing the cinders and fumes from the locomotive to drift into the cars. Passengers had brought food aboard and the aromas from all the different foods intermingled with the laughing, singing and shouting, made it feel like a fiesta. Being an American, in shorts and a tee shirt, my fellow passengers accepted me, especially when they saw I wasn't hesitant in drinking their rum from a jug that was being passed around or sharing the food I brought along.

When the train stopped where we decided to meet at Ciego de Avila, Jorge was waiting for me alongside an ancient convertible. With a big grin on his face, he directed me to jump into the car. We traveled a short distance through the center of town, arriving at the city's port. After parking the car, we climbed onto a small motorboat that was tied up to a broken down dock with one person sitting at the steering wheel.

"Jorge, what's this all about? I thought we were staying in Ciego de Avila for the weekend".

Jorge pointed to an island a few miles offshore, grinned and said, "Avila was only the meeting place. Wait until we get to the real destination, you'll think you're in heaven. I'm taking you to one of my favorite islands, Sol Caya Guillermo, the water is so clear you can see the sea floor at 60 feet".

There were no large hotels, just a few shacks built on the piers over the water and one bar/restaurant on the beach with soft guitar music floating out its open door and windows.

Jorge knew the owner who handed us our room keys. We left our gear in the rooms and went directly to the bar. For the next two days, we did spend time in "heaven".

Sol Caya was a small tropical island you always dreamed about. The beaches were wide and pure white. Blue skies interspersed with big, fluffy, cumulus clouds. Bananas, coconuts, mangos, and pineapples were growing everywhere, all for the picking as were the chaquitas.

When our schedules coincided, we met every few weeks for the next 3 months, travelling to most parts of the Island. On some of these visits, I saw places that the average tourist never gets to see or ever hears about. Jorge was giving me background about Cuba that came from generations of knowledge as well as a wealth of information about business practices on the Island. Most important, my use of Spanish was improving considerably with Jorge's instruction and my practicing with the Cuban employees on the Base. All the information I could give in exchange was what little I knew about the few States I had visited in the United States before I enlisted in the Navy. I described what snow and winter were like only later finding out that he and his family had visited more sections of the U.S. then I ever had and that as children, he, and his sister won trophies skiing in competitions in Colorado, New Hampshire and Idaho.

Our likes were surprisingly similar and the bond between us grew stronger. In serious moments, we spoke about our business futures, but these times were very few. Like most young pilots, getting in and out of trouble in our leisure time was our primary objective, and in more than one instance, several bars in multiple towns were declared off limits to us.

Cuba is approximately the same size as California, and had just as many varying time-off opportunities. Hiking from one town to another, sports fishing off the Cuban coast, watching professional soccer games, or just loafing and soaking up local color in some cantina or casino either on the mainland or on one of the small islands offshore. It was on one of these "just loafing" weekends when he said to me, "Don, the next time we have time off, would you like to meet my family?" They hear so much about the stray Gringo I took under my wing that they're anxious to meet you."

"Amigo it will be my pleasure to meet your family," and with that we shook hands, never dreaming what the future planned for us.

A few weeks later, a visit to his home in Matanzas was planned. It would be an opportunity to meet Jorge's parents, Jorge Sr., his mother, Isabella, and his younger sister, Maria, who was interning to be a doctor and was home that weekend.

Due to all schools of higher education becoming a center of anti-government protests, Batista closed them down. Students who were qualified and could afford it, relocated to the United States and other countries to get their degrees and medical education. Maria fortunately was well qualified on both counts but also had the good fortune through her father's contacts to intern at a hospital not too far from the plantation.

CHAPTER 5

We met at the Matanzas airport, where Jorge was waiting for me in a pick-up truck. I threw my gear in the bed of the truck and off we went. He drove on roads with fields of sugar cane and tobacco growing on each side that stretched as far as the eye could see. I later learned that all this, including the small airport belonged to the Rodriguez family.

After travelling for what I thought was at least an hour, we turned off the road and followed a long, slightly inclined driveway lined with well-trimmed ferns and palm trees. In the distance, I saw the hacienda, located on a small hill, for the first time. As we drew nearer, the Straits of Florida became the background. It was more magnificent than I ever pictured it would be and would be exceedingly difficult even for an accomplished artist to replicate. At the hacienda's entrance, the driveway turned circular enclosing a beautiful fountain and formal garden.

The building was centuries old, two stories high with a belfry at one end where a small church was built into and part of the same structure. Brick and adobe arches supported a roof extending out halfway up the wall making shade and shelter for the tiled walkway beneath it. The windows were all encased in heavy wood and the roofs of the buildings covered with barreled red clay tiles. Later to learn, the tiles were hand made over the thighs of one of the tile makers, then left in the sun to dry before being nailed onto the roof.

The entrance doors were made of carved wood, twenty feet high and hanging from decorative iron hinges centuries old. When the car stopped, one of the hacienda doors opened and a man stepped out. Jorge said, "There's my Papa."

The sun reflecting off the white adobe walls caused me to shade my eyes as I opened the car door and I immediately put on sunglasses.

Jorge Sr. stood ramrod straight, over six feet tall, well-built and tanned from years of being in the sun and fit from physical labor. He had the air of command about him and took me in in one glance as his hand grasped mine in a firm handshake. It was evident that he was a man's man, and a no-nonsense leader of men.

"Papa", Jorge said, "This is the gringo Don I always talk about."

"Don, my Papa, and he really isn't as stern as he looks. He's really a pussycat."

I could feel the love and respect flowing between father and son.

"Welcome to our home, Hacienda Seville" he said. "We have been looking forward to meeting you for some time and with all his upbringing my son still doesn't know how to introduce people properly," he smiled as he said this. Then putting his hand on my shoulder, gently led me over the threshold into their home.

As I walked through the entranceway, the sight was astonishing. The room was massive. The walls and ceilings were of white adobe. Hand hewn wood beams traversed the ceilings and at each end of the room, large arches led into the rooms beyond. The floor was all tiled and hanging on the walls were old Spanish armor, swords, and ancient muskets and colorful serapes tastefully arranged. The furniture was all made of heavy dark wood with some of the chairs covered in tooled leather. The focal point of the room was a fireplace that a person could walk into or in which a pig could easily fit for roasting. At a quick glance, this room with a grand piano at one end could easily hold a party of fifty people.

Going further into the hacienda, I was lead into a drawing room where two women rose from a couch and came towards us. Jorge's dad pointing to the older one said, "Don, if I may take the liberty of calling you Don, this is my beautiful wife Isabella"

As she held out her hand, I found her strikingly beautiful, tall and slender, with a regal air about her. The way she held out her hand I did not know whether to shake, or kiss it. I chose to gently clasp it and gave her the bouquet of flowers I had brought. She accepted the flowers, gently nodded her head and thanked me. I thought she glanced at Jorge Sr. approvingly but I may have been mistaken.

Watching all this, also smiling, was Jorge's sister Maria. From Jorge's description of his kid sister, I did not anticipate the beautiful woman standing in front of me. Was I wrong! Here was someone, almost an exact replica of her mother and only two years younger than Jorge. She too was tall and slender, with jet-black hair and eyes to match. She looked at me and said, "Buenos dias gringo. Bienvenidas a nuestros casa." (Good day, welcome to our home).

Then, looking me in the eye, she launched into a dialog in rapid Spanish, with me trying to catch a word here or there. Finally, Jorge cut in, "Maria, cut it out!"

"Don I apologize for my sister. She gets crazy once in a while, but she speaks English as fluently as we do."

Maria laughed and in perfect English said, "Welcome to our home, gringo."

Looking at me with those sparkling eyes and mischievous grin I could actually feel the energy surrounding her and was immediately taken in by her looks and radiant personality.

That evening Jorge gave me the grand tour of Hacienda Seville. The building was in the shape of a square, with a courtyard in the center. The first floor was for entertaining, cooking, eating, a private entrance to the church, the library, Jorge Sr. private study, and the servant's quarters. The second floor was the living quarters that accessed internally from the first floor or an enclosed staircase in the courtyard that led up to an outside covered walkway on the second floor. Each bedroom had

French doors opening onto the walkway. Jorge smilingly pointed out that if I wished I could leave the doors open and be lulled to sleep listening to the water bubbling from the fountain in the courtyard with privacy assured.

Jorge's home was on one of the largest sugar and tobacco plantations in Matanzas. This land was a Grant from the Queen of Spain in the 1600 hundreds and was given to the ancestors of the Rodriquez family for services rendered in the New World. The Grant extended from the Straits of Florida on the north, to the swamps over the horizon to the south, encompassing thousands of acres of sugar cane and tobacco.

We seemed to be spending more and more time on the plantation. Some weekends, Jorge and I spent all day in the fields with the laborers swinging a machete, digging irrigation trenches, or planting tobacco plants. We ate what the worker's ate, drank from the same water jugs they did, joked and sang as they did and I made sure I worked harder than they, so the "gringo" would be accepted. Finally, Jorge's discharge came from the Cuban Air Force. His family invited me to the formal ceremony at the airbase, and then to a three day "Fiesta" at the plantation. It seemed all of Matanzas came, as did his sister who drove up for the occasion. This accepted "gringo" was introduced to hundreds, accepted by all and felt part of the family and community. It was at this party that I was introduced to Rafael. A very close friend of Jorge since early childhood. The music, like the food, was ongoing but it seemed that every time I was dancing with someone or walking with them away from the house, Jorge's sister kept calling me to help her with things that were inconsequential.

Finally, I said to her, "Maria, what is your problem? Why don't you relax and enjoy the fiesta. You have all the help you need. It's a fiesta for your brother, why can't you and let me do the same!"

Maria had a heart as big and as warm as the Cuban sun, but unlike her mother who always seemed to maintain a calm disposition, Maria had a Latin temper that came to a boil rapidly but just as suddenly would disappear. On this occasion her outburst started in English, drifted into Spanish and after a few minutes, my ears could not keep up with the speed to translate it into

English or Spanish. Fortunately, her mother, Isabella, walked in, started to laugh, then went over, put her arms around Maria, and kissed her. Not understanding anything, I looked at Isabella, shrugged my shoulder, and made a hasty exit glad there were no knives nearby for Maria to throw or dishes to smash. With blazing eyes, Maria looked at me and her parting word as I left was, "Gringo."

Fifteen minutes later, we were on the dance floor where she was showing me new steps in the "rumba" and "samba", her being upset with me and her temper completely forgotten. I did not dare ask her what the outburst was about.

Suddenly the music stopped. Dancers stood still holding on to each other. People stopped eating. Everyone was looking at the bandstand where the conductor was waving the microphone with one hand, and the other, gesturing for silence. Then his voice sounded over the speakers shouting for quiet, when he had everyone's attention he said, "Senors and senoritas, I have an important announcement. Today, December 2, 1956, Fidel Castro has landed on the eastern end of Oriente Province.

The room was very silent, then after a few seconds, a low rumble of voices started that swelled and swelled like a wave building. People started to leave. The fiesta was over.

CHAPTER 6

My Navy Discharge was coming due. Being young, enjoying the excitement of living in a foreign country, totally accepted by friends I have made, and having saved money, I requested that the discharge papers be given me in Guantanamo rather in the States. My mother and sister were doing well, so there was no pressing need to leave the lifestyle I was enjoying. The majority of my spare time was spent at the plantation and I felt very comfortable with the Rodriguez family. After I left the Navy, I was thinking of looking for work in Mantanzas and renting a small apartment near my friends.

On weekends when Maria came home, the three of us and sometimes Raphael, if he could get away from one of his father's radio stations, would take a car and cover miles in all directions finding out-of-the-way restaurants, places of interest or go into Havana for the day.

On one of these visits, the week I was discharged, is engraved in my mind as if it were yesterday. I was sitting on the veranda reading a book, Maria was home and was in the music room playing a sonata by Chopin and Jorge was in the garage working on his car, when Papa stepped out of the house onto the veranda.

"How's the book?"

"It's ok, nothing spectacular. Just something to pass the time until Jorge takes the car for a test ride."

"Don, I would like to have a serious conversation with you," Papa said.

"Si senor," I replied, closing the book and laying it on the table alongside me. Looking at the sea, Papa lit a cigar, turned, pointed to two bamboo chairs on the lawn and said, "Don, let's sit over there and talk. Would you like a cigar or a glass of rum?" I politely refused both, but my mind was racing thinking of what possible direction this discussion was going to take. Then Papa, with a serious look on his face said, "Don, how do you feel about our family? Do you like Cuba? Do you miss the States? Are you planning to return there? What are your plans for the future?"

I was quiet for a time, turning the questions over in my mind and replied, "Sir, to answer your questions: One, I feel as close to your family as if I were born into it. Two, I enjoy the Cuban culture and three, no; there is enough things happening here that I really do not miss the States. I have no immediate plans to return there right now and my future plans are uncertain. Other than my mother and sister I have no ties there, my father died a few years ago."

"Bueno," said Jorge Sr. "I'd like to make you an offer. Now that your obligation to the navy is over, why not work for me? I need someone to develop the export market while Jorge looks after the plantation. Someone we trust, whom we already know and who has become part of the family. You can work with me on Letters of Credit, deal with the banks in New York, hedging in commodities on the U.S. exchanges in sugar and tobacco, to earn, as you Americans say, "Your keep" and if nothing else, it will give you an introduction to international business practices. As for income, I am sure we can arrive at a mutually agreeable sum. I hear that you're looking for an apartment in Mantanzas, which is unnecessary. You have already spending nights here and we sure have the room. By moving in, you'll be close to work and we all feel you're part of the family. I have already spoken to Mamazita, Jorge, and Maria and we all fully agree that you would fit in perfectly. If this is something you would be interested in, we would be honored to have you."

I respected this man for his intelligence and warmth as I would my own father. What he was offering me was so magnanimous, so huge, it was impossible to grasp. I must have stammered or made some sound, because he handed me a glass of rum, and I swallowed it without thinking. He must have sensed the emotion going through me, because he placed his arm around my shoulder as a father would a son. I turned and put my arms around his shoulders, thanked him and said, "May I also call you Papa?"

"Of course you may. Esta bien, it is settled. Let's call everyone outside and tell the family of our new addition but I'm sure they already know."

With that, Papa called the family to the patio, poured everyone a drink and wished health and long life to the new member of the Rodriguez Family.

Jorge was taking on more responsibility learning how to run the plantation. I, learning the ins and outs of international business, and Maria's school schedule was set in a way that she could come home more often. When she was home, the three of us were inseparable.

In my spare time, I developed an interest in why the exterior walls of these ancient buildings didn't erode from the torrential, tropical downpours. I set up a testing lab in a small room in one of the stables. The result was a coating I eventually developed that duplicated the natural waterproofing on the exterior walls of the centuries-old buildings.

Unfortunately I was so involved with what I was doing I took no notice of what was happening around me. The Cuban people were getting more upset with the American takeover of industry in their Country. It was getting more blatant that the American gambling interest in Havana was running Batista and the Cuban Government, hence the Country. Unrest with this situation was always there, but now it was becoming more open and apparent to the Cuban people who were applauding Castro and looking forward to his return. To Batista, the threat of Castro was now getting serious enough to warrant a more forcible crackdown on the supporters of Castro.

Riots occurred in multiple areas all over the country. I started to feel a difference in attitude when I went into town. The people knew me, liked me, but were slowly distancing themselves from anything and everyone American. You could feel the mood actively swinging towards Fidel. Jorge Jr. was talking more about Castro and what he could do for Cuba. In fact, everyone was voicing their feelings but in whispers and always looking over their shoulders when they did. Batista knew what was happening and it wasn't uncommon to hear about some person who had made a casual negative remark about Batista or his government, disappearing during the day or was taken from his bed at night. The Batista followers and one of hope by the backers of Castro felt a sense of fear. The fear of Batista and what he could do in the now, versus the hope of the future if Castro came into power.

The plantation was home, comfortable, and relaxed. The outside political world was of no concern to us. Whether it was studying, lazing around, or enjoying dinner as a family, we were together, yet everyone did their own thing. It was also a pleasant Rodriguez tradition that any member of the family who wasn't present at dinner, there would be a place setting laid out for them, as it was now with Maria not being home. Table talk covered every topic imaginable. In fact, sometimes the conversation became so heated it carried on well past midnight, but no subject or any position caused hurt personal feelings and was never pursued past the dining room table.

The thought of renouncing my American citizenship never entered my mind, but with the average person's feelings about the Americans slowly changing, I didn't want to cause my Cuban family any harm or embarrassment for taking me under their wing. I knew if there was a change of regime, I might have to become a Cuban citizen. In fact, it was apparent that if I went into business or even worked on the plantation, I would have to give up my American citizenship.

With the prevailing feelings against the United States, to be successful in anything would be problematical if you weren't Cuban. I didn't need guidance from my adopted family; I needed acceptance of a decision I finally made after many sleepless nights. That Saturday, after lunch, I asked everyone if we could gather on the patio explaining I had something that was really bothering me and needed them to know of a decision I made.

"You are my family," I started out. "I love you with all my heart but I've been watching what is happening in Cuba and know how some people in the United States have been taking advantage of their position here. For that I apologize, but I cannot do anything to correct it. I have also become uncomfortable in Matanzas by the attitude of people I thought were friends and am concerned that these ill feelings towards me and other Americans may rub off on our family. So far, it's nothing that bothers me, people are calling me "gringo" under their breath, bad service in a restaurant, or ignored, as a customer in a store is becoming the usual thing. Sometimes even some of the people I was doing business with would forget and make a snide remark about the gringos, and then apologize to me for being the exception. The more inroads Castro made, the worse it's going to become and all Americans that live here or love Cuba will be painted as they say "by the same brush". This pressure is the last thing I want for you, or have you exposed to, therefore I decided to return to the States Monday morning until things in Cuba straighten out. Believe me, I've thought long and hard about this and spent many days and sleepless nights thinking it through. I feel it's best for all of us and it seems the best decision for the near future. Please do not think badly of me, or think I'm ungrateful for what you've done or that I'm running. I love you all. You are my family and the last thing I want is for you to have problems because of me."

When I finished speaking the only sound was the breaking of the waves on the shore and the cries of seagulls overhead. Everyone was silent, just looking at me. My mouth was dry and I felt myself trembling. I was deserting the ship. I was sorry I ever opened my mouth to bring the subject up even though I knew in my heart I was right.

Jorge Sr. stood up, walked over to me, put one hand on my shoulder and with his other shook my hand.

"My son, I'm sure you thought long and hard, and spent many sleepless hours thinking through this decision. It hurts me to say this but I understand your position and wish you well. We love you and will truly miss you, the best of luck."

Mamazita put her arms around me and with tears in her eyes, kissed me and said, "Our home will always be yours. Take good care of yourself and I'll say a prayer for your health, welfare and your return to your Cuban home every night."

Jorge, poured rum for everyone and toasted my health.

"Don my brother; I'll miss you as we all will. Fly low, slow, and come back soon and often."

Maria did not say a word just rose from her chair and walked into the house. I followed her in and as I reached her, she turned and with eyes blazing said, "You lied! I thought you enjoyed living here. I thought you were part of this family. Have you really thought this through? You are running."

"Really Maria, you don't understand. Things and times are changing"

"I understand all-right! I'm not stupid nor have I been living under a bush, ignoring what is happening here. I just thought you, Jorge and me would never be separated. Governments may change but not families."

Feeling bad, I innocently put my arms around her. Maria put her head on my chest and started to cry. I could actually feel her body trembling against me. I didn't know what to say or do. Suddenly she looked up, backed away and said, "I guess you're right, I am stupid and acting juvenile. I know what you're doing is right for you, but I'll miss you and the times we could have together."

She walked away and asked, "Why are you leaving so soon?"

"No sense putting it off. If I don't leave immediately, I 'll change my mind about leaving, so it's senseless to put off the inevitable. I already made plans with Jose, the manager's son, to pick me up early so not to inconvenience anyone, and drive me to the local airport. I'll fly to Havana, over to Miami and then take a train to New York."

"Well," Maria said, "I see you have it all planned so since there's no way of changing your mind, all I can say is good luck."

She turned, and went into the study and closed the door behind her. I returned to the patio where the family werc scated and sat down, feeling like a traitor. Jorge Sr., Mamazita, and even Jorge looked tired. I got up and asked if anyone wanted a drink. They said yes, even Mamazita asked me to mix her a cocktail. I poured double shots of rum for Papa, Jorge, and for myself.

From the time I voiced my decision, until the day I left, the mood was somber, and things had changed. We did everything as we did before, but there was a feeling of sorrow, as if someone passed away, over everyone. The joy of being in a vibrant family was gone.

Saturday night Mama and Papa invited all our friends over for dinner. The house was packed with people there to wish me luck on my new venture. I noticed though, Raphael's parents, Mama, and Papa kept disappearing into Papa's study but I was too busy partying to read anything into it.

Sunday, the last day was cloudless, the air filled with the fragrance of tropical flowers mixed with the tang of salt sea air. I went down to the kitchen for breakfast and Maria was the only one there.

"Where's everyone?" I asked.

"Mamazita and Papa went into Havana to see someone, they'll be back for dinner. Jorge is out on the plantation, something to do with irrigation, even the cook went to town. I'll make breakfast and then we'll pack a lunch so you can spend your last day at the ocean," Maria said.

Like an older brother who always teased her, I retorted.

"Sounds good to me. Since when did you learn to cook?"

She looked at me with a young but mature smile and said, "You have no idea what my capabilities are."

Maria packed a picnic basket, added a chilled bottle of wine and a beach blanket.

"It's such beautiful a day, let's put on our bathing suits." she said, "and you can take one last swim in our warm Cuban waters. Then when you are in New York, in the winter, you will wish you were back here."

As she said this, a veil lifted from my eyes. I wasn't looking at a young lady who, over these past two years, I treated and teased as a younger sister. Suddenly I was gazing at a beautiful, desirable, intelligent woman who I cared for deeply. She must have felt my emotion or it must have shown in my eyes. Her beautiful dark eyes instantly turned away from my gaze and her face turned crimson.

When I came down, Maria was already in the kitchen and this was the first time I saw her in a bathing suit. She had the figure and looks of a model. I could not help staring at her and when I lifted my eyes, she was looking at me with a broad grin on her face. I know I started to blush and to cover it up, I grabbed the basket of food and said, "Let's go!"

The Jeep was parked outside the kitchen door and from force of habit, I slid into the driver's side. Turning the engine on, I reached for the short gearshift and the back of my hand accidently brushed her thigh, we looked at each other. I did not know if Maria felt it, but to me it seemed as if an electric shock passed between us. Touching her, as accidental as it was, caused every cell in my body to awaken and it was difficult to keep my eyes on the road and not on her. While it was only a short drive to the beach, the awkward silence was uncomfortable.

When we parked the Jeep, I took the basket from the rear seat, and Maria carried the blanket.

"Don, grab the other end of the blanket!" "Here's a perfect place to picnic with the rocks shielding us from the blowing sand and we can eat without it getting into the food."

As soon as the blanket was spread out and the basket set down, Maria grabbed my hand and with a big smile said, "OK gringo, let's get wet." By this time, my thoughts and emotions were in a state of flux. Holding hands, we ran into the into the water like two children, I was feeling something other than brotherly.

The sea surrounded us like a warm cloak; so clear, you could count every shell on the bottom and see schools of small fish swimming by. We swam, rested and swam back to shore. Then raced each other to where we had left the blanket. There was not a person in sight either on the beach or offshore in a boat. I felt like we were the only two people in the world..... the rebirth of Adam and Eve.

Laughing, wet and happy, we lay down beside each other, but I was far from tranquil inside. The compulsive feeling to stroke her hair came over me. She turned to me and with a force as powerful as two magnets attracting each other, we kissed. The kiss turned to love, love to passion and our bodies melded into each other. With our passions spent, she turned and whispered, "From the first day I met you, I fell in love and today I wanted to be part of you, so you'll always remember me."

"Maria, our lives will always be entwined and as soon as things settle down, I will return and then be together forever."

We lingered on the beach for a short time talking about the future. We kissed one more time, got up, gathered our belongings, and drove back to the plantation. To this day, I feel the same way. We are and will always be part of each other.

Sunday's dinner was gloomy, only the five of us, no guests. Toasts were drunk, tears were shed, well wishes exchanged. I was sure that everyone knew what happened between Maria and me. Even Maria blushed every time our eyes met. Our love was the first love of adulthood, our love was pure, and our love was clean. That last night was torture. Maria in her bed down the hall, her parent's and Jorge's bedrooms between us. I presumed that neither of us slept very well that night, I know I didn't sleep at all. My thoughts were solely about how much time we had wasted and now I was leaving.

Before the roosters crowed, I was fully dressed, went down to the kitchen and made a cup of coffee. The house was completely quiet. Next to my empty cup, I left my Identification Bracelet and a note saying that I loved her very much and was looking forward to our being together the rest of our lives. I would be constantly thinking of her, as I hoped she would be of me every time she looked or touched the bracelet. I blessed the God of Good Fortune that brought me to her and our future together.

It was 4 a.m. Monday morning, Jose was waiting.

Don stopped talking and looked out the window again. Night had fallen and the wind had slowed down. He picked up his spoon and slowly started to stir his near empty cup, staring at the ripples he was making in the coffee. I thought, if only there was a way to capture the emotions that must have been running through his mind at this moment.

He came out of his reverie, looked at me, smiled and continued.

"I felt uncomfortable with the anti-American feelings that were building in Cuba forcing me to leave everything including Maria, but from what I heard Castro was doing everything he promised the people he would do. American companies were being forced out of Cuba. As he advanced, the large American tobacco and sugar plantations were being divided up into small farms, health clinics were opening for the poor, and schools were started. Stories also were being circulated that Castro was getting in bed with the Russians and Chinese, but as of this point in time, nothing has been substantiated."

Don again looked out the window and said, "To go on with my story, I landed in New York."

CHAPTER 7

The plane landed in New York. We offloaded on the tarmac, a short walking distance from the terminal. Snow was starting to fall and I forgot how cold New York could be in the winter. I hailed a taxi, gave him my mother's address and sat back to see what had changed over the past few years that I had been away. The roads were even more crowded and the sidewalks jammed with so many people, I was overwhelmed. A feeling of remorse made me wish that I should have stayed in the land of palm trees and sunshine. The taxi stopped at the address and after retrieving my luggage, I walked to the door and was greeted by my Mother as a "conquering hero son" as all Mothers do, thanking her again for the opportunity of staying with her until I got a job.

New York was the hub for hiring commercial pilots for the airlines. However, though airlines were still expanding as fast as they were an abundance of experienced multi-engine military pilots were available who were given preference over single engine fighter pilots, which is what I was. Finding a job in aviation was going to be difficult.

The savings account I had from my time in the service, plus monies from working for Sr. Rodriguez was my only source of income. After a month of filling out applications and being rejected, I was getting disheartened and beginning to think, that even with the political situation worsening in Cuba it may have been the wrong decision to return to the States.

Then one cold, bleak, windy, and rainy winter morning, the likes of which can only be experienced along New York's East River, fortune finally smiled. I was ordering breakfast in one of the workingman's restaurants on one of the docks along the East River near Wall Street. The wind gusts driving the rain and hail were hitting the window of the restaurant without letup and I was enjoying my scrambled eggs when a well-dressed man, I would say in his sixties, opened the restaurant door and sat down beside me. He ordered coffee and started a conversation about nothing in particular.

"Good morning," he said, "what a miserable day."

"Sure is, a typical winter day in New York."

"You can't be from here. Not with a suntan like that."

"You're observant. I came in from Cuba a few weeks ago."

"If it's not too personal, I'm curious, why New York?"

"Not at all." I was born here and my mother and sister still live in the area. I'm an ex-Navy pilot and this is where the airlines' personnel offices are. Unfortunately my skills don't seem to be needed at this time in the job market", I replied.

"Unfortunately, they're not hiring pilots with single engine time. Flying is what I enjoy and am good at. The only openings are in Brazil for single engine instructors but the maintenance on their aircraft is non-existent, so that is out. This puts me in a bad position. They don't need a fighter pilot for the company you work for, do they?" I asked with a smile. He laughed, "No, I don't think so."

One topic of conversation led to another.

"Tell me about Cuba," he said. "What were you doing down there?"

"I was flying in the Navy and then after discharge was working on a business plan with the owner of a sugar and tobacco plantation."

We started to talk about the politics of Cuba and Castro. He seemed to know a great deal about Cuba and had an excellent grasp of the situation there. Before I knew it, I was telling him about my Cuban family, Maria and our hopeful plans for the future. "Interesting," he said, "you have a wealth of knowledge that only a person living there could gain. Do you know anything about the import-export business?"

"Yes, while I was working at the plantation, my future father-in-law took me into his business. I've done hedging in sugar and tobacco with companies here in the States, and had been overseeing documents including Letters of Credit with New York Banks". I pointed, "In fact two of them are across the Street."

He finished his coffee, got up, and picked up both our checks from the counter.

"Sir, don't do that," I said as I reached for my check. "I appreciate your wanting to pay, but I don't need anyone to pay my bill."

"Nonsense," he said, as he reached out to shake my hand. "What's your name?"

"Don English," I said, and yours?

"Ruggiero, Mario Ruggiero."

"Thanks for the very interesting conversation Don," he said, then half turning he raised his arm, pointed his finger at a building across the street and looking at me said, "I have a feeling paying this check may be returned many fold. Here is my business card, my office is the penthouse. When you finish breakfast, come up, and visit. I would like to continue our conversation and may have something of interest for you."

After he left I looked at his business card. Printed on it was, Mario Ruggiero Investments, along with the address and telephone number. There was no clue to what kind of business investments he was in but if his office was in the penthouse of that building and on Wall Street, it was worth visiting him.

It's said that God moves in mysterious ways, maybe so, maybe it was Kismet, or just plain luck, but within fifteen minutes, I was in a special elevator that only stopped at the penthouse. The door opened into the most opulent reception area I'd ever seen. The room extended out from the rest of the penthouse with floor to ceiling picture windows overlooking the East River on the east, the entrance to New York Harbor on the south, and the Hudson River on the west. A dramatic view even with the rain, hail and low visibility. At the center of the north wall, there was a built in wood burning fireplace making the room warm and comfortable. On each side of the fireplace was a door leading to office wings. The ambience reeked of understated wealth and good taste. Mr. Ruggiero didn't have an office in the penthouse, he had the entire penthouse.

Within minutes after I was announced, I was ushered into Mr. Ruggiero's office. The reception area was well designed, but nothing compared to Mr. Ruggiero's office. The first thing I noticed was that there were no windows. All the lighting was indirect from fixtures in the ceiling and walls. The room was immense and, to me, looked like a replica of a throne room from an Italian palace with dark wood, high back chairs, tapestries hanging on all the walls and a conference table that could easily seat twenty. In one corner was a very large ornate desk, which, I later learned, was hand cut from Carrara marble.

He took a seat at the head of the conference table and pointed to the chair to his right, where we spent two hours talking about the import business, commodity futures, world politics in general and Cuba in particular. In the course of the conversation he explained that one of his companies imported and sold futures in olive oil, while others held holdings in other type businesses. With the problems in Cuba and the shrinking sales of olive oil and olive oil futures in that area, he needed to develop more representation in a sales territory extending from the East Coast west to the Mississippi, and from Chicago, south to New Orleans. I did notice though that other than olive oil, he was not specific about his other business interests, nor did I ask.

The hours had passed like minutes when Mr. Ruggiero looked at his watch and said, "Don, I'm having the chef prepare lunch for the both of us and if you don't mind, let's eat here so we can talk further and you can get an idea of what I need, do you have the time?"

"Mr. Ruggiero, this is the first interesting conversation I've had since being back in New York. Believe me, I have the time."

This was above anything I expected. I never thought of a chef working full time in an office, and was not at ease in a physically enclosed environment like this, but by the time lunch was served I was completely relaxed, yet slightly wary. I knew I was being judged before being formerly offered a job but being dumb, not stupid; I went with the flow, listened and only responded when asked a question. The telephone rang. Mr. Ruggiero picked it up, and while he was speaking, I saw a copy of "Il Progresso" the New York Italian newspaper in his wastebasket. While not Italian, I grew up in a predominantly Italian neighborhood and, as a lark, studied Italian in high school. Fortunately, enjoying the language made it come easy. After studying it for three years and using it on the streets of New York, I spoke and read Italian fluently. Now was hopefully payoff time. I lifted the paper from the basket, raised the newspaper, and started to read the headlines and a few paragraphs on the front page. Out of the corner of my eye, I could see Mr. Ruggiero watching me. He ended the phone conversation, put the receiver down and said in Italian, "Can you read and speak Italian?"

I answered, in Italian, that I studied it in school, and then proceeded to read the article in Italian, finally translating it back into English for him.

He looked at me stunned and then with a big smile, "Ragazzo mio," he said in Italian, "this puts a new light on everything."

He sat back in his high backed leather chair, and, like Papa, selected a cigar from a humidor on his desk, lit it, took a puff, and looked up at the ceiling while he mulled something over in his mind.

"Is your passport valid?"

"Yes, it's good for another three years."

"Would your being out of the country be a hardship?"

"The time would be no problem but I'd like you to explain what your expectations are, so I'll know what I am saying yes to."

"Harvesting of olives starts shortly in Italy. Would you be interested in going there to learn the olive oil business, from the harvesting to the packaging and shipping from Italy to the rest of the world?"

From being despondent this morning about not finding work, to this offer was incredible. Of course, I said yes. We went over salary, travel expenses and all the other mundane things, then shook hands. He called in his secretary, told her I was on the team, to take me to personnel, and introduce me to everyone. As I was leaving, he called me back, shut the door and said, "Don, you report to no one but me, no one, not even my secretary, only me, capisce (understand)?"

"Si io capisco" (I understand), I replied. As we shook hands again, Mr. Ruggiero said, "You start next Monday. Double check to see when your passport expires. The tickets will be waiting for you at Al Italia airlines at Kennedy Airport with an envelope containing everything you will need. Get the feel of Italy and its culture for a week. The harvesting season has already started so you haven't too much time to be a tourist, but if you do a good job, I'll make it up to you in the future.

Bona fortuna." (Good luck)

I replied, "molto graci por tutti." (Thanks for everything).

It was still raining when I left the building but my thoughts and feelings were so different then I had coming into Manhattan this morning, I had no recollection of the walk to the subway station or the ride back to my mother's home.

I could not wait to call Maria to tell her of my good fortune.

CHAPTER 8

Al Italia departed Kennedy Airport, Monday, seven PM and landed at Rome's airport at eight the next morning. After clearing customs, I was looking for a taxi to take me to my hotel, when I saw a man about fifty year's old, holding a sign with my name on it. I walked over, introduced myself and in accented English, he introduced himself as Salvador. He explained that he was to take me to my hotel, be my chauffer, guide, and translator for my entire stay in Italy. Then he said something strange; Mr. Ruggiero was adamant that I never speak Italian or let anyone know I spoke the language. If a person spoke to me in Italian, Salvador would do the translating into English for me. A strange request, but Ruggiero was the boss. Salvador also reminded me never to call New York for any reason other than in an emergency and then speak only to Mr. Ruggiero. My assignment was to keep a written record and on my return give it to Mr. Ruggiero.

Salvador was a treasure. He was intelligent, suave, and very diplomatic. In a few days, we relaxed in each other's company. He mentioned that he lived in New York for a time, and Chicago. With New York as a common bond, we forged a friendship. Why he returned to Italy he never said, nor did I ask. Nor did I ever ask or make notice of the Beretta he always wore in an ankle holster.

More than once in our travels through the various areas of Italy, I was appreciative of his knowledge of not only the different dialects but also the customs, especially as we travelled south into Sicily. His ability with the language and customs were way beyond my capabilities. He knew the best restaurants and places to stay throughout our travels. Another thing he taught me was what vineyard wines to drink in each region. I couldn't wait to impress my new found knowledge with Maria and perhaps share with her all the places I've enjoyed, the people I've met, and the local customs I've learned.

Regrettably, my time in Italy was over and I was going back to New York. Salvador and I had become quite close and even after having several bottles of local Italian wine with lunch, parting was a sad occasion. At the Al Italia gate, we embraced as all Latin friends do, then shook hands.

"Sal, I'll see you the next time you're in New York."

"Don, I'll see you and Maria here when you return. I can't go back to the States. That was one of the conditions why I'm back here in Italy amico."

Nothing further was said. We shook hands again and I went through the gate. Between business and pleasure, I was fortunate enough to have seen Italy from the Italian Alps to Sicily. I called Maria every weekend and went into minute detail as to the areas I visited that week, how beautiful Italy was, how vibrant the people were, and how tasty the food. To her chagrin, our ideal vacation spot changed weekly as I moved around the country.

On my first day back in New York, I went to the office. There were a few people in the elevator with me, who I did not know, and everyone remained silent until it stopped at the penthouse floor. I knew no one, nor did I know where my office was, or if indeed I had one. The door opened and facing me was the only face I knew, the receptionist.

"Good Morning", I said. "Is Mr. Ruggiero in?"

"No, he's out of town but your new office is ready and Mr. Ruggiero wants you to call him at this number as soon as you get settled."

With that, she rose and asked me to follow her to my office. I expected something like one of the other executive suites I saw as we walked down the hallway. She stopped at an office door, opened it, turned to me and said, "Well, here you are."

I thanked her and walked in.

My office contained a desk, two chairs, and a file cabinet. If you stretched your arms you could nearly touch all four walls. The only redeeming feature was that my window faced east and by moving my desk and chairs a bit, I could see La Guardia Airport and watch the planes landing and taking off. My ego deflated like a pierced balloon.

I called Mr. Ruggiero, told him I was back and sarcastically mentioned I was settling in to my new spacious office. Ignoring my sarcasm, he said he was at a meeting and asked if we could meet Saturday morning in the office at about ten. I said it was fine and that was the sum of our conversation. He never even asked me about my trip.

It took me three days, from early morning, before anyone came in, too late at night, after everyone went home, to put my notes in some semblance of order so they would be ready when our meeting took place on Saturday. The report included everything I observed, with diagrams of factory design and machinery, production capacity and shipping schedules, numbers of personnel per factory, the names of the people that gave me the information, and large international buyers. It covered the operation from start to finish; from the harvesting to distribution, and most of all, what improvements could be made, based on my observations and data collection.

Saturday at ten a.m., I walked into the reception room and the first thing I smelled was the deep aroma of Italian coffee. Following my nose into the kitchen, there was Mr. Ruggiero opening a box of pastry with half of one sticking out of his mouth. He swallowed what he was chewing on, put the rest on the counter and said, "Amico, you saw nothing. If my wife found out I'm eating sweets she would kill me. I'm diabetic but I love Italian pastry."

I smiled. Here was a man who must be worth millions and outside of business hours seemed to be a regular guy. He poured another cup of coffee for himself as well as one for me. He looked at me guiltily and took another pastry with one hand and my notes with the other. The atmosphere changed suddenly from friendly to all business and remained that way until he looked at his watch and realized it was noon. Not wanting to spend too much time away from further discussion, he was going to make lunch for us in the office kitchen.

With that, he put on a Master Chef's hat and made us the best shrimp scampi I have ever eaten. The transfer from cook back to astute executive was again incredible. We ended Saturday late in the afternoon, shaking hands after he gathered all the working material, saying that we would continue again Monday. Then, I'm sure reluctantly, but with a smile, he gave me the remainder of the pastry to take home.

The following week we spent a great deal of time together, reviewing everything in minute detail. Around noontime Friday, he put all the papers and notes in his briefcase, thanked me for a job well done and said, "Don you did a great job. The receptionist has a ticket for you for a flight on American Airlines from La Guardia to Miami, Miami to Havana, leaving this afternoon at 3 p.m., take a long weekend. Go see your girlfriend, be back here Tuesday morning. I have something else I want you to get involved with."

I knew he was pleased. I thanked him for his kindness, but felt mystified as to why I was given these jobs when he has people working for him for many years. Why me, kept popping up in my head, but now was not the time to ask. I was on my way to see Maria.

I called Maria immediately and told her about the tickets. She was as excited as I was since she was able to get away this weekend. I gave her the time the plane would land and to make reservations at a hotel near the airport.

Maria met me at the airport late that evening. She looked absolutely radiant and more beautiful that when I saw her last. I opened my arms and she flew into them like a homing pigeon. We got in the car she rented and I couldn't get enough of touching her while she drove, rubbing the back of her neck or stroking her arm. After we arrived at the hotel, I registered as Mr. & Mrs.

The clerk gave me the key to our room, and while going to the elevator, we heard the sound of music coming from the dining room. I looked at Maria and said, "Did you have dinner yet or would you rather freshen up and come down later"

Smiling, in that shy way of hers, she responded, "Why not have dinner sent to the room"?

What a brilliant idea, I thought.

It seemed only hours when Monday came around. Maria had to bring the car back to the rental agency and had classes, so we drove to the airport parking lot to spend as much time as possible to be together. We kissed and clung to each other not caring who was watching us or what they thought as we sat in the airport parking lot. Parting was getting more difficult, so I insisted she drop me off at the terminal rather than wait for my plane to depart. Reluctantly she agreed, knowing waiting would only prolong the agony of parting for both of us. Without her being with me, staying in Havana by myself would not accomplish anything so I caught an early flight back to New York. One thing though that stuck in my mind; She must always be wearing my I.D. bracelet because I noticed that when it rose up her arm, the mark around her wrist wasn't sun burnt, she was wearing it constantly.

As soon as I arrived back at the office Wednesday, Mr. Ruggiero was waiting and escorted me personally into his office. We sat having coffee talking about Havana, Castro, and the sugar and tobacco crops, when his secretary announced over the intercom the men he was expecting had arrived.

"Let them in," he said, and in walked five of the toughest looking men I ever met, big, brawny, and tough looking. All wearing expensive clothes that didn't fit the expressions on their faces. After the introductions were over, Mr. Ruggiero said, "Don, while you were in Italy, we purchased a four-story shell of a building near the docks in New Jersey, and your job will be supervising the flow of building materials and permits for the construction of the building. An olive oil packaging company will move in as soon it's completed so we can't have any unnecessary delays".

I was pleased that he had faith in me, but concerned of my abilities to meet his expectations. I responded, "Mr. Ruggiero, I don't know anything about constructing or building or factory."

"E bene, you don't have to, these men do, they are the general contractors. Your job is to make sure everything they need and can't get, you get. Your job will be mostly labor relations, permits and materials flowing to the site. Meet them at the construction shack tomorrow morning, and by Friday you should know what they need".

"Yes sir, I'll be there tomorrow morning".

I thought, he's paying me very well and being the boss, if that's what he wants me to do, I'll try my best to get it done.

"Bene–That's it. Take the rest of the day off and maybe get some work clothes."

I looked at the men, the men looked at me with no expression on their faces, the looks in their eyes, frankly made me very uneasy and not too eager to get on to my next assignment or work with my new associates.

Riding the elevator down to street level and thinking of our conversation, I decided that I had better check out this building by myself to see what I was getting into before the next morning.

In New York, with the amount of traffic and lack of parking availability, owning a car is an unnecessary luxury, taking a taxi is more convenient. Therefore, I hailed one, gave the driver the address in New Jersey, sat back, and enjoyed the ride through the Holland Tunnel. A construction fence surrounded the building and fortunately, there was a trailer parked outside with a security guard, who after I identified myself, let me onto the site.

The building was four stories high and completely devoid of any floors, windows, or doors. It was just a shell of a building with a roof. In the rear of the building was a small canal leading into the lower Hudson River and rusted railroad tracks leading to a loading dock. My curiosity was satisfied by my ten-minute survey and I was committed to tomorrow morning.

The building was built in record time, even with the shortage of certain materials and labor, due to the booming economy. While not exactly following the blueprints, the result exceeded the specifications and was more like a fortress whose floors could hold five times the load the prints called for. This was done with the acquiescence of the building inspectors.

At least twice a week, to keep in physical shape and to the amusement of my associates, I would change from a suit to dungarees and work shoulder to shoulder with the men digging ditches and doing masonry work. My knowledge of the Italian language and its dialects changed from pure Roman to Sicilian. Every lunch consisted of submarine sandwiches and cheap red wine, surrounded by the unmistakable and distinct aroma of "Lupos", the Italian cigar. I never smoked, but to this day, I love the aroma of those cigars that bring back many pleasant memories. I wonder if "Lupos" are still being manufactured? A month after the building was completed, after the city's inspection and approval was given, an olive oil company did move in. My learning curve in heavy construction increased ten-fold, and would help if I ever decided to open my own business. I never went back to see the facility in operation nor did I ever think I would see my mentors in construction again.

Mario Ruggiero and I spent a lot of time working together. In retrospect it was not boss and employee, nor was it father and son as it was with Jorge Sr.. To this day, I cannot put my finger on what our relationship was. While warm and friendly, he was sometimes cold and withdrawn. I never felt completely relaxed and always felt there was a secret part of him I could not reach.

There was gossip around the office that Mr. Ruggiero had a son about my age and a younger daughter. He never spoke about his family nor were there any pictures of them in his office or on his desk. In idle conversation, the receptionist said neither his wife nor children had ever called or visited the office as long as she had been working there and that she employed there for more than eight years. His photo appeared with many influential people in the newspapers, as he was a large contributor to political parties, the New York Opera, and symphony, and a multitude of clubs and associations. There was no evidence of this on the walls in his office or on his desk, just as there was none of his family.

For the length of time I was employed by him, my position had no title other than, "Trouble shooter". I accompanied him on trips to building sites, conferences, kept a check on olive oil sales to our accounts in the eastern part of the United States, overseeing Letters of Credit and keeping him abreast of the commodity markets throughout the world. He was a tough competitor in business, always made sure to have an edge, and usually won. I remember the time he bet me fifty dollars that within a week, I would buy a tuxedo.

Mr. Ruggiero won! He never mentioned that I was going to accompany him on an overnight trip to California where he was backing a movie and needed someone he could trust as a witness to a meeting.

Even though I enjoyed the hands-on experience, I was getting with Ruggiero's construction projects and business dealings, there was still something missing. Everything I did seemed to fall into place, as if the pathway were paved for success and always ended to his satisfaction, but it wasn't giving me the personal gratification I was seeking.

As the saying goes, "I was living high on the hog", making an unbelievable amount of money for someone in their twenties but, while gaining an enormous amount of business knowledge, I felt a change had to be made. Then one day I had an epiphany. We were looking over the foundation of an office building he was constructing when it came to me. Concrete building foundations need waterproofing and block and brick walls absorb and allow driving rains to go through them. Why not go into my own business with the product I developed in Cuba?"

The country's economy was doing well and going into my own business was getting to be a stronger driving force, a compulsion to do something by myself, for myself. I needed to put my new found skills to work for me. Since any business decision I made had to include Maria's and our future, I phoned her and asked if she could meet me in Miami at the Fontainebleau Hotel for the weekend. A decision like this had to be done in person, not over the telephone. Because of our long distance relationship, her life and mine were in the same state of flux and things had to change.

The weekend at the Fontainebleau was everything we both hoped it would be. Our bodies were not strangers to each other. When we made love, it was soft, fulfilling, and complete. We spoke of my intended business venture, Maria's career, and how it would affect both our futures. Our decision was that when my company was financially carrying itself we would marry and Maria would finish her medical education and training in either Cuba or the States. The day turned into night, night into day and like a beautiful white cloud, driven by the wind, the weekend evaporated. Maria returned to medical school and I back to New York to give notice to Mr. Ruggiero and start my company.

Now back at work, after the wonderful time spent with Maria and still wanting the freedom of working for myself, I kept putting off speaking to Mr. Ruggiero. Finally, with much trepidation I asked his secretary to set up an appointment with Ruggiero.

"Hey kid, what's with this formal appointment? You usually knock and walk right in."

"Well, this is a serious matter and it means a lot to me, so I wanted it to be more formal," I said.

"This does sound serious. O.K., then let's keep this strictly businesslike, and you sit across the desk from me."

"Mr. Ruggiero you taught me a lot and I appreciate everything you did for me but now (I felt myself stuttering and starting to perspire) I feel I have to see what I'm capable of by going into my own business."

He looked at me, his facial expression without change and he uttered one word, "Why?"

"I developed a product in Cuba that proved to be an effective waterproofing coating. With the construction business growing as rapidly as it is, with the proper marketing, and contacting the right architects, I know I can build a profitable business.

He held up his hand to stop me.

"How old are you", he asked followed by, "and how much have you got in the bank to start this venture?"

I told him the sum, but as I mentioned the amount, I realized how small it was to start a business, but once I said I was leaving, I now had to resign, if for no other reason than to save face.

"Don," he said, "You're doing a good job here. You don't need to go into business any more than you need to get married at this time. With the casinos closed in Havana, the American public will be looking for other places to vacation and throw away their money. They are not only visiting casinos in the Bahamas but are buying property there for future development. Why do you think we're buying properties in Louisiana, Mississippi and along the East Coast. The future and real money is in building and controlling casinos. Stay with me for five years and you'll be lighting cigarettes with $100 dollar bills. I will not stop you from leaving, if that is what you feel you need to do, but you're young and have your whole future ahead of you. You are very capable and I would like you to stay with me. From where I sit, you are making a big mistake and making this call by emotion rather than intellect and I'm talking to you like my son".

I had committed myself! Taking back my words was impossible.

Mr. Ruggiero used every ploy to keep me on board, but my mind was made up and my decision made. No matter how good the money was, I was not working for myself. Finally he shrugged his shoulders, went to the wall liquor cabinet, opened a bottle of Champagne and poured two glasses.

"Here's to your health and your new venture," he said lifting his glass.

I raised mine and said, "Here's to both our health and fortune," in Italian.

"Mr. Ruggiero, now that I'm leaving may I call you Mario?" He laughed.

"Sure my young friend. I am going to miss you but remember this, and remember it well, what you saw or think you saw, or heard or thought you heard while working here, was only in your head. It was only a figment of your imagination and that is where it stays. capisce?" We shook hands again.

I stayed to finish the week and complete some assignments I had. When I walked into Mario's office after saying goodbye to the few people I knew and as we shook hands he pressed an envelope into my hand.

"Don, you're making a mistake, but youth must have its way, so good luck and keep me posted as to how you're doing. My only suggestion is open your manufacturing business in New Jersey, not New York."

While in the elevator, descending for the last time, I opened the envelope and was amazed at the amount of the check in the envelope and for a few seconds, wondered if I made the right decision.

Only months later did I realize that Mario's suggestion of opening the business in New Jersey was the best advice I could ever have received. Many of the people that left the olive oil business went into different phases of the construction industry along the East and Gulf Coasts and their building sites could easily be reached from New Jersey.

What I didn't know was that they remembered me and were giving my company business without my knowing it because of past business dealings. A handshake was more sacred than a contract and my word to deliver was never in question. My initial investment in addition to Mario's check, was sufficient to give me the holding power I needed to put me on the road to eventual success.

The biggest problem though, was the ongoing political turmoil in Cuba. Castro was steadily making further advances west of the Sierra Maestra Mountains of eastern Cuba against Batista's forces. There were also growing rumors that Fidel was getting increased advice, as well as, aid from Russia and China.

However, Fidel Castro and his campaign in Cuba had not touched Maria or me, as yet.

CHAPTER 9

With my business growing, I had time to visit my Cuban family, with Maria, in Matanzas or at her Aunt Clara's house in Havana when she could get away for a long weekend. The few times the family was together, I would bring up their moving to Miami and their retort was always the same; they would not think of it. Their home, their heritage, their wealth was too much to leave behind and the thought of selling their assets was far beyond their scope of possibility. As with most older people, emotionally tied to the past, hoping things would get better sometimes is unrealistic, but their constant response was that eventually things will turn out all right.

On one of my visits to Matanzas the three of us, Jorge Jr., Maria, and I, were sitting on a rock ledge watching the low swells of the Florida Straits hitting the sea wall.

The tang in the salt air on the ocean breeze felt cool and took the heat of the summer sun off our tanned bodies. It felt great to be home.

"So Jorge," I said, "Since your dad is talking about retiring soon, you'll be taking over the plantation. What do you think the future holds?"

"Problems," he replied.

"There's already talk that when and if Fidel ousts Batista, his plan is to cut up estates and other large holdings, and giving the workers small farms. Sugar cane cutters and their families have been with us for generations and have been treated fairly, but realistically, who knows what ideas can be planted in their heads since it's human nature to envy the boss and what he has. Little do they know the risk of weather, markets, payroll, and taxes. How true the old saying, the grass is always looks greener in someone else's yard." Everyone would be pleased if Batista leaves but it is not worth your life to say anything openly or even hint it, since you never know who is listening. The American fruit and tobacco companies will be forced to leave, and if they cut up the plantations into small farms, with no supervision, no money for fertilizer, no harvesting machinery as the American companies have, I am afraid that the granjeros (farmers) will fail. Who knows what will happen to the original landowners and what is in the future for them, if everything is nationalized.

Then Jorge slowly looked up at the blue sky, then at the incoming waves, and across the plantation that stretched to the horizon. To me it seemed he was absorbing and committing to memory everything for the first time. He turned back to us and continued, "Don, you heard the rumors that Fidel is possibly getting backing, as well as ideas from Russia and China and it may be a good thing. They're also saying that these countries are already promising him millions in exchange for Cuban sugar and tobacco. If he gets into bed with them, Cuba may be lost; Castro will be like a child playing baseball with a seasoned professional. On the other hand, it may be just the thing to help untangle the financial ties to the United States."

Holding my hand, Maria was just sitting there listening to the conversation, absorbing all that was being said.

"What do you think Maria?" I asked.

"The only good thing I am hearing is that Fidel will institute universal healthcare, even for that, we have to wait and see. Healthcare, primarily of babies and children is the only thing that interests me, politics do not. Hearing of the advances being made in the United States by my friends who left medical school here and being trained in the States, makes me envious of what's happening just a few miles North of us and has opened my eyes to how backward Cuba is in training doctors. Maybe, and I sincerely hope that under Castro things will be better. They sure can't be any worse than they are now."

Jorge and Maria then turned to me and asked for my opinion.

"I'm not an authority on economics or politics, but a few days ago, I was amazed to read in a Havana newspaper, an article picked up from a Miami source. It stated that's it's publicly known that profits are being skimmed off American companies and casinos here and being sent to banks in the States and Switzerland by Batista and his cronies. When I read it, it seemed to me, a dangerous thing for the editor to print at this time, and would only be adding fuel to the fire and putting his life on the line. The next morning on Radio Havana, it was reported that a gang of unknown hoodlums entered the newspaper's office during the night, destroyed all the presses, and set fire to the building. The police had no clues as to their identities."

"My own thoughts are that the more inroads Castro makes, the more turmoil there is going to be in Cuba."

I flew to Cuba to celebrate Papa's birthday. Maria was home a few days before I arrived. She picked me up at the airport and seeing her again reminded me of how lucky I was. We had decided that this was the right time to announce our wedding plans to the family, on the same day we celebrated Papa's birthday. Sometimes though, events overshadow plans and expectations.

Papa's birthday dinner was always served on the lawn. The house could not accommodate the number of people that attended. There were ten linen covered tables set in a U shape. Each table seated twenty people, each table was set with crystal glassware, and hand fired plates. I later learned that a pottery maker on the plantation made the plates. At the end of each table, there was a bar set up with every type of liquor, wine, soda or juice imaginable, served by two waiters in tuxedos. Off to the side were six pigs roasting on spits placed there last night. Children sat at their own tables supervised by young girls from the plantation. Family, friends, plantation workers all mingled with ease and from what I heard this was one of Hacienda Seville's yearly rituals since Jorge Jr. was born; the other being Christmas.

After dinner, Jorge Sr. tapped on his glass for silence, rose, and then gave a toast for health and good fortune to all. After everyone sipped from there glass, Jorge Sr. again tapped his glass one more time, and when everyone quieted down said, "I have another announcement to make. I am getting on in years and want everyone to know, including my son Jorge, who knows nothing of what I'm about to say that as of tomorrow I'm turning the entire running of the plantation over to him."

All eyes turned to Jorge. Everyone started to clap their hands or hit silverware against their glasses. Jorge's face showed the amazement and surprise he felt. A few moments after it sunk in, Jorge rose, went over to Papa, embraced him, and then turned to the assembled.

"Papa I appreciate all you have done for me and what you just announced, but before I accept, I'd like to talk to you alone."

The room immediately turned silent. Even the children, sensing something, stopped running around. Papa's face turned ashen as he looked at Jorge not understanding what he heard then looked at Isabella. Their eyes met, and she slowly shook her head and lifted her shoulders as if she also did not understand Jorge's request. Family members started to talk among themselves, not knowing why Jorge did not immediately accepted his father's generous offer.

Then Jorge Sr. held up his hand for silence, everyone quieted down. Facing his guests and family, Papa stood proud and said, "I will speak to my son tonight, and let you know his decision tomorrow. It is my birthday, let us enjoy it."

When Jorge made this unexpected announcement, Maria looked at me with tears in her eyes. I knew immediately what she was thinking. This was not the time to make public our wedding announcement. Our happiness, our lives, were on hold until we knew what Jorge's plans were.

The talk that night was that all Americans would be thrown out of the country when Castro came to power. The Batista government was already asking foreigners to think about leaving for their own safety. I again begged the family to come to the States. Their lives were more important than their assets. Anyone who read a newspaper, listened to the radio or even rumors on the street knew trouble was brewing and if possible, it was best to leave Cuba for a time and return when things normalized, as did so many who were now living in Miami, including Rafael's family.

That night Jorge spoke to Papa after everyone left, and they again had a meeting early the next morning in Papa's study. The mood later at breakfast was very somber, then Jorge looked around the table at us and quietly said, "I decided to join Castro and I'll be leaving in a few days. I feel that anything will be better than Batista. While I'm not in full accord with some of the rumor floating around, I feel as Fidel does that, Cuba is for Cubans and there will be no ties to any foreign country after he comes to power."

We all tried to dissuade him, but like Papa, once his mind was made up, there was no turning back. Papa just sat there looking at Jorge, with tears in his eyes and looking his age. Even his shoulders, normally thrown back and proud, were slumped in defeat. Mamazita was dabbing at her eyes and in the last few minutes seemed to age. Maria sat very still, looking at Jorge in disbelief. She turned to me, hoping for an answer, but there was none. Knowing Jorge as I did, I got up from my chair, went over, shook his hand, and wished him good luck. As soon as Maria and I were alone we jointly decided to put our wedding plans on hold until Jorge returned.

Castro's army was moving closer to Havana and things were getting more chaotic for the Cuban people. In the larger cities and towns, random gangs were roaming the streets looting indiscriminately. Any business either owned by an American or thought to be American, was pillaged, and burned. Utilities were functioning only part time. Both Castro's and Batista's forces had first choice of gasoline or diesel fuel for their vehicles. Foodstuffs were rotting in the fields due to lack of transportation. Train or plane schedules were nonexistent. Americans and Cubans were leaving Cuba in droves, as they became aware their lives and fortunes were in jeopardy.

The day after Papa's party, I flew back to the States. We were so involved in our careers that our only contact was a weekly phone call but we did manage to see each other, at Aunt Clara's house in Havana, in what turned out to be our last time together. Our plan, at the time, was also to visit her parents in Matanzas but the political state for an American traveling within Cuba was too dangerous to even attempt this short trip.

As Castro was "liberating" Batista's Cuba, some people realized he was reneging on all the promises he had made when he was still up in the mountains. His appointed block captains to oversee the comings and goings of all persons in the area and to report any unusual actions to the authorities. Expressing any anti-Castro opinion was at your own risk. People were being taken to prison in the middle of the night, for no known reason. Some were shot, no different from under Batista's rule. Getting rid of his opposition was supposed to solve all the problems. His tactics were a foretaste of what the future would be like when he arrived in Havana. However, all this was kept under strict censorship from the areas yet to be "liberated".

For some reason, once she was interning, Maria's calls to me were getting more infrequent and my calls to her were not all being answered and when they were, they were brief and I felt something wasn't quite right. Sometime after Papa's birthday party, I received a letter from Maria saying that she was now in Havana, after being selected to develop a new program for interns in Cuba that would revolutionize the medical educational process. The offer was presented to her by a doctor at the hospital where she was interning and she was accepted by the doctor heading up this program in Havana. The entire thing was secretive and she couldn't tell me about it, until now. She had decided to complete her internship in Havana. She was sorry it was so short a notice, loved me and hoped to see me again.

There was more but I was so taken back, I put the letter down, picked it up again and reread the first paragraph over at least a dozen times. The rest of the letter went on to say that Jorge had passed through Matanzas for a day. He was thinner, more introspective, less spirited but still with the determination of a conquistador. Jorge told the family he carried a rifle in the Sierra Matera Mountains alongside El Jefe (Castro) where they ate, slept and fought together for freedom from Batista and the American interest that controlled the island. With Fidel in power, Jorge did not think things would be as the people expected. Papa asked Jorge to expand on this, but Jorge just shook his head and said, "Wait, time will tell."

Who knows what the future holds, All my love.

Maria

Within the month, all telephone communication and mail were now being censored or monitored by the military. To insure the health of the Cuban people, it was mandated that medical personnel were no longer allowed to exit Cuba under the penalty of imprisonment. Both the U.S. Government and the Cuban authority's now made visitation between the two countries impossible.

Calls to and from Maria and my Cuban family, were now non-existent. I tried through various Consulates in Havana but they could do nothing for me. My dreams of a life with Maria was now nothing but a fantasy unless I could, in some way, get her out of Cuba. Then the question came into my head. With all she has going for her in Cuba, would she want to leave. Someway, somehow, I had to find out.

Rumors were rife that Castro was a communist, and while he vehemently denied it all the changes he was making in Cuba later proved to be dictated, formulated and supported by the influence and leanings of Russia's Khrushchev.

January 1, 1959:
Batista, his family and close associates board a plane at Camp Colombia to leave the Island. Che Guevara and Camilo Cienfuegos lead the rebels into Havana.

January 2, 1959:
Manuel Urrutia is installed as President and Jose Mira Cardona as Prime Minister.

January 7, 1959:
Castro arrives in Havana.

January 11, 1959:
Throughout the Island firing squads start eliminating, "war criminals".

February 16, 1959:
Fidel Castro, Commander of the Rebel Army, replaces Cardonas as Prime Minister of the Revolutionary Government.

April 15, 1959:
Castro visits the United States as a guest of the American Society of Newspaper Editors.
Says he is not a Communist.

June 4, 1959:
In Cairo, Che Guevara makes the first official contact with the Soviet Union.

October 15, 1959:
Raul Castro becomes Minister of the Armed Forces.

January 18, 1960:
The CIA creates the Cuba Task Force and begins a draft version of what becomes, "A Plan of Covert Action Against Cuba".

February 6, 1960:
Soviet Deputy Minister Anastas Mikoyan arrives in Havana resulting in a trade agreement with Cuba.

March 17, 1960:
President Eisenhower approves a covert action plan against Cuba including the organization of a paramilitary force of Cuban exiles to invade the island.

CHAPTER 10

It was nearly a year since I'd heard from Maria. No matter what avenues I tried, no one could help me contact her. Reading the daily newspapers was my only source of information as to what was happening in Cuba and the results were unfortunately exactly as I had forecast. It was reported by the fortunate few that did escape Cuba, Cubans attempting to communicate between the two countries were doing so at the risk of being imprisoned or shot.

One clear, cold, sunny morning, sitting in my office daydreaming of being with Maria on a white sandy beach in Cuba, my private telephone rang. A man introducing himself as John Smith said he was calling from Washington D.C. and without preamble immediately asked if I could meet him for lunch at the Federal Building in Manhattan the next afternoon. The word," scam" immediately popped into my head.

"Hold on," I said, "I have someone on the other line."

That was a lie but I needed a few seconds to clear my mind that started travelling at warp speed. No one had this unlisted phone number other than Maria. The only thing I had to do with anyone from Washington D.C. was with the I.R.S., and my company had only been audited a few months before so that could not be the reason for the call. For someone to specifically come up to New York from Washington made me uneasy.

"What's this about?"

"It's important, and I rather not say over the phone."

"You're giving me no insight into the subject and want me to meet with someone from Washington? How do I know this isn't some con game, and how did you get this unlisted telephone number?"

"Getting your number was easy; I'll tell you more tomorrow," the person replied.

The caller must have heard the suspicion in my voice.

"If you need to verify this call, let me give you this phone number, extension and my name, simple as that. Does that meet with your approval?" he asked.

"O.K." Let me have it."

"Ask for John Smith, at this number and extension.

I hung up; very dubious, waited a few minutes, then placed the call.

The telephone operator answering just said, "Washington D.C." No Department name or other identification to indicate where my phone call was being routed to, but within seconds I had John Smith on the line. I still was uncertain of what he wanted but after speaking for a short time, reluctantly agreed to meet with him the next day in New York. He gave me the address of the Federal Building. We firmed up the time and he suggested I ask for him by name at the receptionist desk in the lobby. The receptionist would give me further directions and would be escorted to his office.

On the way to the appointment, it came to me, that maybe I should have taken my accountant or attorney to sit in. As in all Federal Buildings, there were armed guards at the receptionist desk checking I.D.'s and briefcases. I gave her my name and told her I was expected by a Mr. John Smith. She made a phone call and informed me a security guard would be with me shortly to take me to Mr. Smith's office.

The guard arrived, escorted me to the elevator and accompanied me to the fourteenth floor where I was handed off to another receptionist and another armed guard. I was asked again for identification, then followed a guard to the most mundane, unattractive office I have ever been in.

It had light tan walls, no pictures, a desk bare of any papers or even writing equipment, fluorescent lighting fixtures hanging from the ceiling and two chairs; one behind the desk and one in front of it. It looked more like an interrogation room than an office and to my eyes the only thing missing were handcuffs and electrodes. I felt uncomfortable but more curious than concerned. What could happen? I was in a Federal office building in the middle of Manhattan.

The guard left and no sooner did he leave than the door reopened and in walked a man dressed in a dark suit, white shirt, black tie, and a severe look on his ruddy face. He introduced himself as Mr. Smith, shook hands and asked me to please sit, while he placed a well-worn briefcase on the desk as he sat down.

Our eyes met after sizing each other up. We were about the same height and weight. He looked about ten years older than me and must have spent a great deal of his time outdoors, judging by his suntan and the wrinkles around his eyes. His hair was pure white and to me, he looked and dressed like a college professor teaching in some Ivy League college or a mortician.

There are many ways to break the ice with a stranger. One can start a conversation about the weather, sports, or some other mundane subject. There are also times, such as now, to prudently keep your mouth shut and let the other person steer the conversation so you will know what the subject is and where it is going. This to me was one of those times.

"May I call you Don?" he asked.

"Only if you tell me your name," I responded

"It's John," he said." I thought I told you its John Smith."

"What an unusual name, John Smith," I responded with a smile.

"Any relation to the John Smiths of Virginia or New England?"

We both knew the answer to this and both smiled, so I continued, "Well John I'm delighted to know you. but tell me why am I here and why is the government buying me lunch?"

He never answered my question. Instead he smiled, opened his briefcase and began reading some documented information about me. Some, of which, I hadn't thought about in years; school records, Navy records, clubs, people I knew, people I did business with, bank records, even back to the time my ancestors emigrated from Ireland, the date they landed and where they settled in Massachusetts.

"I'm impressed, and damn angry. This is an invasion of my privacy. I never imagined that the government kept such close tabs on its citizens. I thought this went out with the McCarthy era," I said as I stood and walked to the door, turning the knob to open it.

"Hold on Don. Come back and sit down. I apologize for not explaining but because of what we need to discuss, I had to do a background check on you."

He put the papers back into his briefcase, stood, and said, "Let's have lunch."

In seconds, his attitude changed from being an interrogator to a pal. The last thing on my mind at that moment was food, I just nodded. The only thought in my head was where was this conversation going and not lose my temper. I was more confused now than when he called yesterday.

This Federal Building has its own penthouse dining room the likes of which only taxpayer's money could maintain. The room was attractive. Everything was color coordinated, the décor reminiscent of an old English Men's Club. As soon as we walked in we were escorted over to our own reserved table overlooking New York City. The Federal Building was built decades ago, and was now surrounded by buildings much, much taller than this one. All you viewed were surrounding office windows. Apparently, there was outdoor dining for use in warmer weather. The trees and bushes were bear since we were now in the middle of winter. All the outdoor tables and chairs were covered with tarps. Fortunately, we were eating in the heated dining room. Our table was away from everyone in its own alcove, a place secure from any prying eyes or ears.

We ordered and Mr. Smith got right to business. He lifted up one hand, then, as if he were counting fingers, saying, "One, you like to travel! Two, you have friends in Cuba! Three, you flew in the Navy! Four you know small boats! Five, you speak Italian and Spanish and you have friends in certain circles of the business world. Am I correct?"

I shrugged, why affirm, or deny anything at this point of the conversation.

"What you don't know and are unaware of, is that some of those old friends are giving you business as well as the government. That's why your business has grown so rapidly."

"Hold on", I object to your statement that I'm being fed work. I have a good product that's accepted by the construction industry and saving thousands of dollars for the contractors."

"Yes, you have a good product and it has been well received, but where did you think much of this business comes from? Think about it, geographically your big contracts are from the Eastern seaboard, Gulf States and companies holding prime government contracts. Who do you also know in these areas?"

My mind quickly flashed over the last few years and the contracts I had. He was right, but I was getting upset. My ego was being deflated. My mind was in overdrive trying to find a retort but I couldn't come up with anything. In addition, not only was my ego bruised, my lunch was turning to acid.

"Look, let's cut to the chase. Why am I here?"

John Smith looked at me and said, "We have been following your travels and business career for a while and like you, would prefer to see some changes in Cuba. It's possible with the people you know or knew, that you can help bring the changes about."

"Who's this we"? I asked.

"Our group," he said.

"And the name of this group?"

"Really Don, what's in a name? Just our group."

My brain swirled with unanswered questions.

"Look, if I weren't somewhat connected," he said, "I would never have access to the information I read off to you. If I weren't connected, we wouldn't be eating in this dining room. So let us just say we would like you to work with us at times. I cannot give you any guarantees, but let me say this, if you help us, and if there's any way we can get Maria and her family out of Cuba, we'll do our best."

The mention of Maria and her family suddenly brought me to attention.

"What do you know about Maria and her family?"

"Unfortunately, not too much," he said.

"O.K., I'm still not sure but let me hear what you have to say."

"What I'm about to say, stays here, agreed and do I have your word?"

"Of course," I mumbled, "you seem to have me over a barrel."

"Castro isn't what he appears. He's courting both China and Russia, and we think he is turning communist or already is. If he does, Cuba will end up a dictatorship ninety miles off our coast and if one of those countries establishes a base there with missiles, we are in deep trouble, as will be the rest of Central and South America, especially Panama and the Canal. With your business background and connections, you could be an asset in helping the Cuban people."

With the thought of all the hard work that was put into building my company, no matter how business was coming in; I did not want to see the rug pulled out from beneath me. Nor picture myself a James Bond, but the thought of being with Maria and the family, once again, was primary in my thoughts. Also knowing the power of the Government; to close any corporation down at any time and or give out government contracts, could lead to the success or failure of any business. I was boxed in and John Smith knew it. He looked at me and smiled. "When do you need an answer?" I asked

He pushed his chair back and said, "I need to know the beginning of next week and if you are onboard, we will meet in Virginia, I'll be expecting your response."

"Oh, order anything else you may want and stay as long as you wish. The check is already taken care of."

As he was walking away, he stopped, turned and said, "I nearly forgot, there is something else."

He reached into his jacket pocket and pulled out an envelope.

"I believe it's from an old friend of yours," he said as he handed it to me.

I took the letter from him. There was no writing on the envelope other than my name.

"John, did you read it?"

"Of course," he said, and left.

It was a letter from Jorge dated a month before.

Mi Hermano, (My Brother), I'm sending this through a trusted friend so I needn't be too careful as to what I write. The Army came to our house, told papa and mama to move out, that they were taking it over, and forced all the help to leave. My parents broke down and pleaded to stay. Papa went to Havana to protest and is now in prison. Mama is living with her sister until things are sorted out and I feel very helpless. Apparently, Maria is oblivious to what is happening and dedicated solely to her medical career and Castro's regime. My hands are tied. I found a job crop dusting and dropping insecticides but the government is smart. They only give you enough fuel to do the job but not enough to fly across the Straits. I have become a common thief, and am stealing gas from cars, buses and any other vehicle that runs on gas, storing it away so when the time is right, I can top-off the aircrafts fuel tanks. Then, my friend, I'm Florida bound. If and when, I make it, I got your telephone numbers from Maria and will meet you in Miami where I'm joining a newly formed Cuban Resistance Movement, which I understand Rafael is part of.

Abrazos (with affection), Jorge

The letter, as John Smith knew it would, made up my mind.

I stayed in Virginia about a month handling business by phone, and with John, going over maps of Cuban ports, intelligence reports, design of boats, and the availability and use of weapons. Then after "graduation" which consisted of John buying me dinner at an excellent restaurant in Norfolk. I returned to New Jersey where my company was located. In checking the books, my business did not suffer, on the contrary in my absence both the gross and the net profits increased.

CHAPTER 11

Months passed without hearing from Mr. Smith, but many times when a plane was passing overhead from Newark Airport, my thoughts drifted back to my Cuban Family and how, not too long ago, one could get on a plane and fly to Cuba with ease. Did Maria miss me as much as I did her? Was Papa still in prison? Was Mamazita in good health and was Jorge still crop dusting?

As I walked into my office one morning, my unlisted phone was ringing, I held my breath. The only persons having this unlisted number were Maria and John Smith. I lifted the receiver hoping to hear Maria's voice, when I heard a male voice on the line saying, "I'm calling for John Smith. He asked that you meet him at the DuPont Hotel in Miami, tomorrow at two p.m., your tickets are at the United's counter, Newark Airport. Your plane leaves at seven in the morning.

That was it! The line disconnected. No hello. No regards from John. No goodbye, just a disconnect tone.

As I approached the reception desk at the DuPont, waiting for me stood John Smith, still dressed like a mortician in Florida's heat, but with a big smile.

"Hi Don, good to see you again."

"Hi John, I'm not quite sure it's good to see you again."

"Well, hold off judgment until you meet some people I have waiting for you."

"They must be important people to have me fly down here on such short notice."

He placed his hand on my elbow and steered me down a long corridor of rooms, stopped at one and knocked. The door opened, and facing me was Jorge. Looking over Jorge's shoulder I could see Rafael. John looked at me with a big grin on his face, as was Rafael.

"Even though it's not December, here's my Christmas present to you Don. Jorge will tell you how he got here. It looks like the Three Musketeers are together again."

Jorge and I just looked at each other for what seemed an eternity, not believing we were actually together again. After entering the room, we grabbed each other around without saying a word, bombarded by a multitude of emotions, tears unashamedly in both our eyes and running down our cheeks. We both started to speak, each stopped to let the other go first, and then both started talking again. Holding onto Jorge's arm, I turned to Rafael, "Come over here you bastard and join the party. Yes, the three Musketeers are together again."

Between the laughing, joking, singing, and noise in both Spanish and English, I'm sure if John had not taken over, an occupant of one of the other hotel rooms would have called the police. John finally stood up, made the universal "stop" sign with his hands and said, "Guys you can continue the party later but now let's quiet down and get into the serious discussion of why we're here. The most important thing, and this remains in this room even though I'm sure it's expected by Castro, is that the U.S. is training a force of Cubans to return to Cuba's soil. We need boats to see how intensive they are guarding their twelve mile limit offshore, and if the Russians are participating with ships or planes. To do this we are getting boats manned by volunteers like you and giving them a sector to patrol. Since you volunteered to do something for the cause, and if you're still committed, just say so, and meet me at the Chalk Seaplane ramp on Monday at 8 a.m."

We all nodded, he shook our hands, and thanked us. John was sensitive enough to know it was the appropriate time for him to leave.

After a few hours, Rafael excused himself saying he had a family waiting dinner for him and would see us tomorrow.

Now that Jorge and I were alone, I started to flood him with questions. First and foremost about his parents and Maria.

Jorge looked at me, became emotional, with his voice cracking, and told me what happened.

"Papa has been in jail now for months for crimes against Cuba. No one can get in to see him under any circumstance. I don't understand Castro or this regime; nothing is as it was supposed to be. The Rodriguez family always financially, helped the poor and contributed heavily to educate the underprivileged in Cuba. I volunteered to fight Batista under Castro's banner and now after all that and generations of giving, our name means nothing. Our home, our plantation has all been nationalized. Mamazita is living with her sister, Aunt Clara. Maria is now a doctor in Havana. Our family and our name are reduced to less than nothing in the, "New Cuba.""

"But," I asked, "Now that Maria is a doctor, can't she use some influence to at least to get in to see Papa?"

"Don, you don't understand! Cuba today is a dictatorship and they're flush with power. Even if you walked into Havana with Castro, as I did, you have no assurance you will be alive tomorrow. Everyone is jockeying for power, and until everything settles down it is best to lay low. Maria says she is trying, and I believe her, but getting to the right people, or finding who the right people are, seems to be impossible." Jorge then grinned.

"Don, I think you should hold on to the arms of your chair. With all our problems, there is one ray of sunshine."

"There is? Enlighten me."

"I have something to tell you that's very important."

His grin turned into a big smile.

"Come on Jorge, spit it out."

"Don, you and Maria have a beautiful son, Maria named him Eduardo."

I looked at Jorge. The words were not fully registering in my brain. I have a son!

I'm a father? When I fully comprehended what Jorge said, my first question was how does Maria feel and who was with her when she gave birth. Strange, I felt sad for not being at her side, but pleased we had a son together that tied us for the rest of our lives. It must have shown on my face because Jorge grabbed my hand.

"Hermano, by leaving Cuba, you did what you had to do and history shows it was a wise decision. Maria is well and so is the boy. Everything will turn out the way it is planned in heaven. Let's toast to your son Eduardo and to the health of our family."

A few hours later, because our reunion was emotionally exhausting, we decided to call it a day. Jorge was going to call Rafael and tell him we would meet tomorrow for lunch at the Cuban diner on Calle Ocho, in Little Havana. After Jorge left, I stayed the night in my room at the DuPont. It is impossible to describe all the emotions and thoughts that went through my head and what I was feeling. Maria and I had a son! I'm a father!

The next morning, I hired a taxi to take me to the diner. The driver dropped me off and I could see Jorge and Rafael already sitting at an outdoor table. As soon as they saw me, they called the waiter and I had a mojito waiting for me before I even sat down.

"Ola Papa", they both said in unison. "Sit down old man and let's talk". For a short time, we reminisced about the times we spent at Nestor's in Havana and the trouble we used to get into. Then the idle chatter turned serious. We discussed what living conditions were like in Cuba and the number of people leaving any way they could. We still did not know the reason John had brought us together, but we surmised that it had something to do for the betterment of the situation in Cuba.

At that point, Rafael took over the conversation.

"Well amigos, if you remember at Papa's birthday party, we had told you we had already sold the radio stations to the Americans and I was just helping out the new announcer at Pinar Del Rio before leaving for Miami. Under Batista, Cubans still had some free speech, but my parents, having gone through this before, knew that free speech under Castro was not going to be possible, just as it had been under Franco in Spain. That night we tried to get Jorge's parents to sell everything and join us in Miami. We told Jorge Sr. of all our plans, to open a bank, go into construction, buy land, and suggested he be part of a new life. Jorge Sr. would not consider it, saying he could not give up the family's heritage and believed everything would be as it was, and nothing would affect the Rodriquez family. The decisions your parents made, as he looked at Jorge, unfortunately put them in the situation they are now in."

Jorge and I looked at each other; we remembered it all too well. Rafael continued, "Jorge, Don, my father knew what he was doing. It is the best move we could make, both financially and for security reasons. I'm happily married, have two children, own a home, and have a growing business. My father was right not only about leaving Cuba but also by starting a small bank to finance Cubans that come to Miami. We are not only loaning money for Cubans to buy homes but we are now in commercial loans and may be starting a construction and development company soon. The future in Miami is getting brighter and brighter every day for us and knowing my father, he will be thinking of politics next. The door of opportunity to leave Cuba is long gone. Now we need to try and give true liberty back to Cuba."

As a cloud could cover the sun on a beautiful day, a shadow fell across our table. All three of us looked up, there stood John.

"Hey, don't mind me; I don't want to break up your party. Glad to see you three so relaxed. Take the rest of the weekend off and I'll see you Monday."

With that, he turned and walked towards a waiting taxi. I caught up with him and as he started to open the car door, I asked how he knew where we were? Ignoring my question, with his big smile, he slid into the taxi's seat and said, "Oh Don, by the way, we've already spoken to your CPA. We are putting in a manager to oversee your business while you're away so it runs as if you were still there."

Before I could respond, the taxi door closed. Something was beginning to trouble me. Both the radio and newspapers were reporting that an anti-Castro group, supported by the U.S. Government, was being formed and trained in the Everglades and Central America. I began to feel that I was involved in something deeper and bigger than I realized.

Shortly after John left it started to rain. Rafael had errands to do and left.

Jorge and I walked into the bar, found two deep chairs in a quiet corner and Jorge continued to tell me more about what had happened since I left Cuba.

Don opened the straps of his briefcase as he was talking; he pulled out a thick book.

I stopped recording. Don asked, "Do you need another tape in the recorder?"

"No Don, but if you're tired we can continue tomorrow."

"Tired?"

"Not at all. It's a relief having someone to tell my story to, so let's continue, but first let me tell you about this diary", he said as he held it up.

"I started this diary the first day I knew I was getting involved in our government's relationship with Cuba. This is a daily record that documents everything that happened by events and dates. I must have read it over a thousand times and I relive every day with all the joy and pain it brings back. This is the first time in years it is out of my house. If there's any part you need to use as a reference, feel free to do so."

"Now let me tell you about Jorge".

CHAPTER 12

JORGE'S STORY

Miami Florida

The bartender put two mojitos on the table; Jorge looked at me, took a deep breath and started his story.

"Don, let's go back to the day you left for the States. When the family came down to breakfast, you were long gone. Mamazita pointed to the note under your empty coffee cup addressed to Maria with your ID bracelet lying on the butter plate. We were sad that you made the decision to leave because of the negative sentiment that was developing against Americans but happy for you for doing what you thought was right."

"Maria had tears in her eyes with a few unashamedly running down her cheeks. She immediately put on your ID bracelet, folded the letter slowly and excused herself from the table as she dabbed her eyes with a napkin. It was apparent that you both truly cared for each other and we all felt and hoped the future would bring you back together."

"I called our friend Rafael and suggested he and I meet for dinner that evening, since we hadn't seen each other for a few weeks and I needed some male companionship. As you already know, Rafael's family owned several radio stations on the island, and our families knew each other since Rafael and I was in private high school. We were also roommates at the University, took the same courses, played on the same soccer team and graduated at the same time. If you recall when you and I became friends, I introduced you to Rafael and in a short time, everyone thought that we bonded like the Three Musketeers and took it for granted that where one was, the other two must be close. Rafael, our profound thinker, Don the adventurer, and me, the rich man's son. When you left for the States, Rafael and I started to drift apart. Rafael spent more time at the radio station. I started to spend more time at the plantation. I guess your leaving was our wake up call to grow up, each of us in his own way."

"Rafael and I met at Nestor's, our favorite haunt, the small restaurant and bar at the waterfront, unknown to tourists, where local fishermen were the principal customers. When I arrived, Rafael was already seated at a table."

"Ola Rafael," I greeted him as I came in. "Que pasa? You're getting as fat as a gringo since I saw you last."

"Ha, my skinny friend. You can work out in the sun being the machismo hombre swinging a machete, I'll take my cool office looking at the senoritas all day, doing nothing more difficult than speaking into a microphone to my radio audience."

He pushed a chair out from under the table with his foot and said, "Sit! I already ordered a mojito for you."

Do you remember the place Don?"

"Sure, I can picture it in my mind now. The last time we were there, three sides of the building were open to the sea breezes with the roof covered in palm fronds."

"Well Don, everything was the same as when we used to go there. The tables, chairs and bar all handmade of bamboo by Nestor. He was still the owner, still as ancient as his guitar and strumming his favorite tunes composed by Lacuona in the '20's." His wife, Lenora, was running the kitchen with their children.

Some people with courage teased him that Lacuona were the only tunes he knew how to play. You had to admit that he was a professional with a guitar and few knew that he and Lacuona grew up together. Nestor never was pretentious. The food was always exceptional, the drinks well made, and the open ambiance looking out on the Straits of Florida were ideal for relaxation and conversation."

Rubbing his eyes, Jorge said, "Anyway, to continue my story."

I thanked him, sat and said, "What's happening on the home front?"

"Well, rumor has it that Castro has moved deep into the Sierra Maestra mountains. Batista isn't saying anything about it at this time, but I know that he's moving troops to that area and is starting to clamp down on news reporting, not quite censorship yet, but I can feel it coming if things aren't nipped in the bud shortly. My father's contacts are saying that things are going to get worse.

Between you and me I'm very concerned."

"Rafael, our families have known each other a long time, and we have no secrets from each other. Let me ask you a question. What do you think of Castro?"

I lowered my voice. We both looked around at the tables filled with people, especially the tables nearest us. We put our heads closer together, and he whispered, "Jorge nothing can be worse than Batista and the American Mafia running Cuba. Not a day goes by that I can't say something negative and factual about Batista but don't dare say it over the airwaves. The entire Havana population knows his bagmen visit every hotel, casino and nightclub daily collecting his pound of flesh, which is immediately deposited in Miami and Swiss banks. It is no secret! Even the clerks handling these transactions joke about it. If all the pledges Castro is making about cleaning things up, and keeping the money in Cuba is half-true, we would all be better off with him. Forgetting Batista and what he's stealing for a minute, think also of the American companies and what they are taking out of Cuba. Let me give you some facts my friend."

"Wait Rafael, before you get me more depressed, let me buy another round of drinks."

"Ah my rich, cheap amigo, since it's so seldom you do, the waiter is right behind you."

The drinks were served and Rafael continued.

"In 1956, American Interests owned 90% of the Mines, 80% of the Public Utilities, 50% of the Railways, 40% of Sugar Production, and 25% of Bank Deposits. We are living by their rules here in Cuba. They pay our labor what they want. There is not a position above a field laborer that is held by a Cuban. Every management position is held by a gringo. Even in the casinos, you have the Americans behind every gambling table with the Cubans cleaning the toilets. True, Cubans own small retail stores, but here again, the Mafia controls by having Cuban gangsters collect protection, which is then split two ways. Jorge, my dear friend, something has to change. The American government knows what's happening here, but their eyes are blinded. They are being controlled by lobbies and laws made by payoffs to their Congress, and possibly, political contributions made by the Mafia."

I sat back in my chair. Nothing Rafael said was new, or what I hadn't seen or experienced personally. We had been dealing with some of these American companies for years. They tell us what they'll pay and there's no dickering with the price, plus the fact that under Batista's law, we can only sell to the Americans and not on the open market.

"So Rafael, what do we do?"

"Jorge, I'll tell you what my family is doing, but keep this to yourself."

Rafael leaned closer still and said, "The family decided that if more censorship is imposed and not knowing the results if Batista stays or Castro wins, we are in the process of selling the radio stations and our properties to some American company so we can get top price in American dollars, no paper, closing to be in Miami, and our family moving there."

"Our family has been in Cuba since we left Spain when Franco was taking over also by force just as Castro is doing now. It seems that the only stability in the world is the United States. With all its faults, it's the only place to live and invest. Why Miami? Simple!

Because of the Latin population already living there. We feel that if any further problems develop in Cuba, Miami, because of its closeness and Spanish speaking, will be the first place Cubans will start to migrate to. They will need banks for loans and will naturally gravitate to us. My parents suggested your family join but your dad feels that Cuba is his home no matter what happens. Also, and again this stays between us, we heard that Castro is not everything he professes to be. There's a rumor that if Batista and the Americans are thrown out, that Russia and or China are waiting in the wings to align themselves with Castro."

I sat back in my chair trying to assimilate all this information, including the real possibility of losing another friend, Rafael, to the United States.

"So Rafael, when is the family thinking of putting the stations up for sale?"

"We already have a tentative contract on everything. The closing and money transfer will be in Miami next month and if everything goes as expected, so will we.

By the way, I feel Don did the right thing going back to the States. The present feelings towards Americans preclude him going into any business in Cuba. There will be trouble in the not too distant future and being American isn't going to make it any easier."

Rafael was very intelligent and being in the information industry, he and his family were "in", and with the political and business contacts they had, I respected what he was saying and what his family was doing. They were intelligent enough to leave Spain when the situation with Franco was similar to this. Cuba to them was only a stopover, not a home. Maybe they were right, but Cuba was my home and I had to decide what I was going to do to keep it my home.

We didn't realize how fast the time passed until the sun began to sink in the western sky. The afternoon breeze started coming off the Straits, mingling the tang of salt sea air with the smell of Nestor's fried fish. Some of the fishing boats were already tied up to their piers and a few had their day's catch laid out on the concrete sidewalk waiting for buyers. To add to the background of the restaurant's clattering pots and pans, the sound of hungry seagulls filled the air, adding to the symphony following the fishing boats back into harbor.

Our conversation occasionally turned from being serious to the crazy times the three of us had together. We both wished in our hearts that everything was going well for you in the States. After one more Mojito, Rafael, and I looked at each other and each knew it was time to part. We rose at the same time; put our arms around each other's shoulder, then with a handshakes said, "Hasta luego" not knowing when or if we would ever see each other again.

CHAPTER 13

"The family received a letter from you every two weeks. Some arrived as if they were opened, some did not, we wondered if censorship had already been imposed. Your letters let us know how difficult it was trying to get a job and we all felt that we were part of what you were doing and what you were going through. Maria received one every week. Here again, some opened, some not. Of course, she never shared most of what the letters contained with us, nor did we expect her to. The days she came home from the University, after kissing everyone hello, her first request was "Any mail for me?" I started to kid her about her relationship with you and never knew my sister could blush".

"Within the month, several important things happened that changed my life. Castro was making tremendous inroads on his march to the capital. It was rumored that the population was feeding him and his troops voluntarily and more people were joining his ranks. Also rumored, when confronted by Batista's forces, most of Batista's soldiers joined Fidel without him firing a shot."

Jorge continued, "In Havana things were ugly and getting uglier. People that were known to be anti-

Batista were put in jail and some say, shot. Trials by juries were cancelled and martial law declared. Anyone even suspected of being pro-Castro were sentenced and shot the same day. Armed Batista guards were placed in and around the casinos, hotels and nightclubs with weapons loaded with their safeties off, with orders to shoot anyone causing trouble. Censorship of all newspapers and radios went into effect. Sympathetic pro-Castro students were immediately expelled from the University or disappeared. Fortunately, Rafael's family closed on their sale and was in Miami two weeks before this happened."

Jorge stopped speaking for a few minutes, and took a sip of his drink.

"Do you remember Papa's birthday dinner when all the family and friends were together, and Papa announced he was turning the plantation over to me?"

"Do I remember? I said. Did you know that was the night Maria and I were going to announce our wedding date? We didn't when you said you wanted to speak to Papa before accepting the plantation."

Jorge looked at me. His eyes opened wide. He reached out his hand as if to ward something frightening away.

"My god Don, I had no idea. If I knew that, I never would have said anything."

"Jorge, its past history, please go on."

Jorge continued looking at me. Tears started to form at the corners of his eyes. I could see he was very upset and did not know what to say. I reached over the table and covered his hand with mine.

"Hermano todos estan bien" (Brother everything is O.K.), I said.

He took a breath, wiped his eyes on his sleeve, let out a deep sigh and continued.

"That night, Rafael's parents begged my father and mother to sell or leave everything and join them in establishing a small bank in Miami. They kept refusing to even think about it. Their response was the same response you got when you brought it up. It was that Papa felt Castro was or was not the answer to everything.

He was too proud to leave the land his family had owned for hundreds of years. My thoughts were entirely different. I felt Cuba needed a drastic change."

After our guests left, Papa called me into his study and said, "Jorge, you're a man and a man should do what he feels is right. After Mama and Maria go to bed I would appreciate your joining me on the patio.

We haven't had a man to man talk in a long time."

"Si Papa, I'd like that very much. You know I respect your thoughts and I'm sure you can give me insight into many of the questions I have."

So, cooled by a gentle breeze, with a full moon painting the Straits of Florida a pale yellow, and the sky alive with stars, I joined Papa on the patio. We sat in our favorite chairs, as Papa poured two glass of rum, lit his cigar and said, "It's no secret that in November of 1956, Castro and 82 Cuban revolutionaries boarded a broken down yacht named La Gramma in Mexico and headed for Cuba. Seven days later the yacht ran aground near Los Calorados beach in Cuba's Oriente Province. The landing was well south of the force's link-up, where fifty supporters awaited their arrival. Government warships patrolled the coast and government planes flew overhead. In fact I never asked but your squadron could have been one of them. Surprise was not a factor; there was none. Three days later, soldiers surrounded the revolutionaries almost annihilating them, with only twelve of the guerrillas surviving and escaping into the Sierra Maestra Mountains to continue their fight against our ignoble President, Dictator and strongman, Fulencio Batista. People of that area, especially the Guajiros always believed that people from Havana looked on their city, Santiago de Cuba, as backward, the people ignorant and always exploited by the Havana government. In addition, because it was so far from Havana they felt that Santiago de Cuba was shut off from Havana as if it were another country. Throughout Cuban history, these Guajiros were always proud, defiant and anti-government with Santiago de Cuba the starting point of every Cuban Revolution. Castro needed them."

He stopped for a few moments, took a sip of rum, took the cigar out of his mouth and looked at the glowing tip. In all my twenty six years of knowing my Papa in every situation as a husband, father, businessman I've never seen him as upset as he was this moment. He took another sip of rum.

"Hijo (Son), would you mind continuing our conversation before breakfast tomorrow morning. I 'm so tired of thinking. All I want is to get a good night's sleep. I think I'm getting too old to fight this world."

"Si Papa, Get some rest. You have a lot on your mind and need a clear head.

Tomorrow before breakfast will be fine. Oh, to keep the record straight, my squadron wasn't involved with Castro's landing."

Early the next morning we met in his study. He seemed more rested and cheerful compared to last night. Papa picked up where he had left a few hours before.

"Castro was intelligent enough to recognize and exploit these qualities using the Sierra Maestras as his operational base and set out to win and encourage the Santiagueros' support of his revolution. He recruited them, and had them inform him of any government action in the area or any stranger entering the rebel zone. See Jorge, I have my own sources of information. I'm giving you a history lesson and telling you things you may not know, but there is another important issue at stake. It's imperative you know, understand, and are aware of what I'm saying. Our family has, by the grace of the Spanish Throne, along with hard work and good fortune, been here for over 300 years. We survived under everyone that came to power in Havana, including Batista and the Americans. There is a rumor, now listen carefully, only a rumor, that Fidel has communistic leanings. If this is so, in every country that has been taken over by a communist regime, large landowners like us are the first to go to before the firing squad. If you want to join him, so be it, I wouldn't stand in your way. We will be concerned about your safety, so keep your ears and eyes constantly open. When you can, let us know how and where you are."

We finished our coffee, I thanked and hugged him, and then we went into breakfast where Mamazita and Maria were waiting for all of us to sit down together.

At breakfast, I told Mamazita and Maria my plans. In a few days I was going to join Castro on his march to Havana, saying, "As a pilot without a plane I wouldn't be of much use, but I could handle a rifle as well as anyone.

Mamazita and Maria both started to cry. Even Papa had tears in his eyes, but my mind was made up. I had to do what I felt I must do.

The next day I called several friends from my former squadron to have lunch and see what additional information I could possibly learn. They were able to give me an idea of where Castro's forces were located. Between flying and camping over the Island for years, knowing the approximate area to find Castro's forces was not so difficult, but to evade Batista's forces, I had to plan it like a military operation. A few days later, my map was mentally drawn and after a hearty breakfast with the family and a few tears I kissed everyone goodbye. I promised I'd write, put my backpack on loaded with some dried food, clothes, pens, pencils, writing paper, and left. If Batista's soldiers stopped me, as I was sure I would be, I was ostensibly a freelance writer doing research and writing background articles for foreign publications about the Guajiros; who they were and how they lived, these illiterate black, white and mulatto peasants of the Sierra Maestra Mountains. Cubans knew most of the Guajiros were squatters who cleared land for subsistence farming and built huts in which to live between sugar harvests. During harvests, they left their mountain homes and worked as sugarcane cutters. Castro understood that to survive in the Sierra Maestras he needed the independent Guajiros and for the first time the Guajiros were getting what someone promised them. Fidel's words were being transformed into action and served to steel the resolve of the Guajiros to support the rebels. The network of these people kept the rebels informed of the presence of not only Batista's troops, but of any stranger who entered the rebel zone. Therefore my road to Fidel was through the Guajiros.

After a year of fighting Batista's troops, Castro was half-way across the Island to Havana, so with nothing more than my backpack and good walking shoes, I did something I never attempted before; I jumped on a slow-moving freight train heading east until I thought I must be close to where the fighting should be. I had yet to hear the sound of an exploding shell or the sharp crack of a rifle. The train slowed, and then stopped to put water in the locomotive's boiler, but overhearing the trainmen's conversation with someone told me the train was returning to Havana rather than continuing east. Fortunately, I could see a road leading to a small town well within walking distance. After jumping off the boxcar, I followed the road, for the next two days, hitched rides on farmer's trucks and horse drawn carts until I was at the base of the Sierra Maestras, and had yet to see a soldier of either Batista or Castro. I was now in Guajiro country.

On the third night, it happened. I was sitting outside a make-shift lean-to. The night was still; clouds covered the moon with the only light coming from a small cooking fire in front of me. My thoughts were of how appreciative I am now in taking that required course in survival while in the air force. It was deathly quiet when I felt a cold, round object against my neck.

"Don't move amigo, if you value your life. Who are you and what are you doing here?"

I anticipated being approached since I had had the feeling I was being watched for some time but I was startled by the stealth and unexpectedness of it.

"My name is Rodriguez. I have no weapon senor. I am a writer interested in writing a book about the Guajiro and have come a long way."

"Put more wood on the fire, so I can better see you," he said.

I did, and after looking me over very carefully, he tied my hands behind my back, and then patted me down looking for a weapon. Not finding one, he pointed to an animal trail with his flashlight and ordered me to walk. I asked him several times where we were going. His only response was to shove a rifle against my back to keep me moving.

We did not walk far. Perhaps 500 meters where the trail opened into a small clearing. A good number of men were gathered around multiple campfires. Between the light of a full moon, and the campfires, I could see that they must have been living in the bush for some time. Many wore uniforms, some wore civilian clothes, but all were dirty and ragged looking. Each had either a rifle in his hand or one close by. The air was filled with the pungent smell of smoke from meat cooking on an open fire with the sound of swarming mosquitos everywhere. Prudently, the entire encampment was sitting downwind of the smoke from their fires to escape the mosquitos.

"What have we here?" asked a tall, thin man walking towards us, no better dressed than the others. From the little military experience I had, I knew from their grouping while at rest, closeness to their weapons, and the layout of their tents, that they weren't a ragtag bunch of Guajiros, but were the rebels I was looking for.

"I've come to join your group and fight Batista," I said.

He unceremoniously emptied my backpack on the ground, looked at me and said, "How are you going to fight Batista? The sharpest thing you have are two pens and three pencils."

Everyone within earshot, including me, started to laugh. At least this hombre had a sense of humor. I explained that I flew aircraft for the Cuban Air Force, and was now out of the service, but saw the need to volunteer to fight Batista and give Cuba back to the Cubans.

"Well maybe I believe you. We can sure use all the help we can get, so take some food for yourself, get some sleep in one of the tents and we will talk more in the morning."

He took out a knife and cut my bonds.

"Unfortunately your hands will have to be re-tied after you eat amigo, but if you're who you say you are, I'm sure a few hours till dawn with your hands tied shouldn't prove too big an inconvenience. On the other hand, if you're not who you say you are, your hands being tied will make no difference since when the sun comes up you'll see your last Cuban sunrise."

I must have checked out to their satisfaction. How, I have no idea. The next morning at breakfast, he came over, introduced himself as Gomez, untied my hands and asked if I knew anything about radios and did I speak English. When I said yes, he told me to gather my belongings; we were marching to a small town in the mountains named "Hombrito" where Fidel, Raul, and "Che Guevara" were. They needed a radio operator who was Cuban and bilingual, as I was to communicate in Spanish to the local area, and in both languages to a widening audience, primarily the United States, as we progressed towards Havana. The humor dawned on me as he said this; If Rafael were still in Cuba, I would be in radio announcing in competition with him to see who had the largest audience. On the way down the mountain and on rest stops, Gomez was constantly referring to "El Hombrito", our destination.

After hours of walking, a rest period was called. Addressing Gomez, I said, "Gomez, what is this Hombrito you constantly refer to?"

"Rodriguez, you have no idea of the planning that went into this entire venture of Castro. When you see Hombrito it will give you an idea of his intelligence and the far sightedness of people like Raul and Che."

He continued, "Some time ago, Che Guevera asked and received Castro's permission to build a small scale infrastructure in his sector of the Sierra Maestra, a small village named "El Hombrito". Guevara's action demonstrated to the local population the rebels' commitment to improving the Guajiros' lives. He built a small hospital, a bread oven, a pig and poultry farms, a sugar factory, a cigar factory and paid farmers to grow certain types of vegetables. He also started a small newspaper that was copied on a mimeograph machine with articles by himself and Castro to illustrate their ideology and their plans for Cuba's future. Batista also targeted the Guajiros but not in appositive way. With the strength of Castro's campaign, government inroads into the rebel zone were prevented. Castro gave the Guajiros hope and the Guajiros gave Castro the time, support, and protection he needed."

I thought back to what Papa said and how right he was. How did he, living in Matanzas, figure out what Castro was going to do six hundred miles away in Oriente. Even with all the contacts Rafael's parents had, with radio stations over most of Cuba, they said nothing or knew nothing about how important the Guajiros were to Castro and how Castro needed them on his side. Time for sitting and resting was over. We got to our feet, picked up our gear and moved on down the mountain to our destination.

Late in the afternoon we arrived at the base of the mountain, and there spread out before me was the complete small town, "Hombrito". As if ordained by a higher power, the fleecy white clouds were now being replaced by dark rain clouds, thunder was rumbling over the valley and lightening started to streak across the sky. It did not start raining yet but the air was thick and the slight breeze that was rustling the dense foliage a few moments before was now still. I instantly thought this must be an omen of things to come. Before I could absorb what I was looking at, I was standing before "El Jefe" himself. Fidel was an imposing figure, over six feet tall, well built, dressed as he always was in army fatigues and as everyone pictured him, puffing on a cigar. His eyes seemed to look through you, but they were always moving as if seeking something beyond your conversation with him.

"Tell me something about yourself," he said.

I started to tell him about my Air Force experience, but he cut me short with, "I know all about that. Tell me more of what you know about radios."

"Well Commandante, as we flew newer model aircraft, we had to take more courses to qualify in radio and radar transmission and reception. I'm very qualified with the latest Cuban communication equipment".

"Diga me (tell me), I understand you may speak English fluently."

"Si senor."

"Where did you learn it?"

"Everyone in my family is bilingual. We have many American friends, did business with them here in Cuba and Miami, and I took advanced courses in English at the University."

"Your father owns a big tobacco and sugar plantation in Matanzas, no?"

"Si senor."

"What does he think of you being here?"

"He's not involved, nor were we ever involved politically with any party."

"Esta bien." (ok). He looked at me as the attorney he was. We both knew, he knew my answers before I answered any of his questions.

The Rodriguez's family was well known and my being in the class of Cubans that he was trying to overthrow possibly made him hesitant about giving me the job of operating the short wave radio. Never the less, after travelling all the distance by boxcar and then through the mountains, I had nothing to lose. So I said, "Are your hesitating because of my background or my experience with radios?"

"A radio in a plane or on the ground is still a radio. They both operate on the same radio waves and frequencies, and besides, it may be that you may not have anyone here that speaks Spanish and English fluently as I do."

I don't think he had anyone speak to him like that, but he was intelligent enough to know the truth of what I said. So after staring at me for some time, he said, "Esta bien" (ok) we will try you."

I was led into a hut that had a sizeable antennae standing alongside it and he asked me to read the printed script over the air in Spanish. Basically, it was a tirade against Batista and his troops, telling the people about the rebels' success and what he will do when he takes over Cuba. Then his plea, in English, to the U.S. was not to get involved. He was building a democracy in Cuba that had nothing to do with the communist or Russia. Apparently, my reading went well. I was assigned the position of radio operator and was told that every statement read, had to read exactly as printed and only from Fidel or Che Guevara. I had just read the prepared statement saying that Russia was not involved and yet the equipment that was being used for transmission was new and had Cyrillic markings stamped into the metal frame. Maybe my father was right; it was not a democracy he was forming, but had more of a tendency toward a communist state.

Over the months my suspicion about his ties to Russia and communism were becoming more and more apparent. Castro and Guevara were excellent strategists and knew the use of propaganda and political warfare. Raul, a younger brother doing nothing but following on the coattails of Fidel. Guevara and I disliked each other from the time we met. To me he was a snake that would turn on anyone with or without provocation to further his cause toward total communism. This campaign helped them gain Cuban society's favor and prevented an international (specifically American) reaction to the insurrection and ultimately the rebels' victory and defeat of 30,000 well equipped Batista soldiers. My thoughts and suspicions had to be kept to myself since I could not dare say or hint at what I felt, heard, or saw. However, even with ambivalent feelings, I believe in giving credit where credit is due. Castro was a born leader, Guevara, a born strategist. My best example was when we surrounded the town of Mompi, which was under the control of Batista's forces. Castro had planned a brilliant propaganda campaign.

A perfect example would be, the next morning Fidel had an aide come to escort me to his tent. When I got there, Fidel, Raul, and Che were gathered around a map of Mompi and as soon as I entered, their conversation stopped.

"Rodriguez", Castro said, "I want you to read over what I wrote and we're going to start broadcasting this as of 0600 tomorrow morning to the Mayor of Mompi.

Another transmission is going to be in English to the gringos. So, your job now is to translate the Spanish into English, comprende?"

I did as he asked and for five days, fifteen hours a day, Fidel had me broadcasting both in Spanish and English guaranteeing the Mayor, if he surrendered his troops, all the soldiers would be treated well before being turned over to the Red Cross. At the end of the fifth day the Mayor surrendered the town.

True to his word, Castro kept his promises. However, I knew the planning behind his generosity from overhearing his talks with Raul and Che. They did nothing without planning and the planning always had some propaganda benefit as one of the targeted result.

His humane treatment of his prisoners of war served to legitimize his fighting force in the eyes of his adversary as well as the world. As Castro's army marched across the island, Batista's military commanders could not rally their troops to fight the rebels. The troops chose to desert and join Fidel.

Sundays no one works or fights in Cuba, so we relaxed in camp. We saw an American touring car slowly winding its way up to our compound, trailing a heavy cloud of dust from the dirt road. Every so often, it would blow its horn twice, as if it were signaling or announcing its arrival. Fidel came out of his tent, as did Raul and Che from theirs, gathering in the middle of the road, awaiting its arrival. As the car came to a stop, a uniformed Cuban driver stepped out and opened the rear door for a tall, portly American who was dressed in a white suit, white shirt and tie, white shoes and a white Panama hat. His face was flushed from the heat, and as he stood there waiting for Castro to walk over and greet him; he kept wiping the perspiration from his face and neck.

After standing immobile for a few moments, he realized that Castro was not walking to him, so he decided to make the first move and walked over to where they were standing. No one shook hands or even smiled. Fidel seemed to know who he was and beckoned to him to follow as he turned and walked into a tent. Raul and Che stayed outside. For several minutes loud voices could be heard, the loudest being the American.

From what I could gather, the subject was about money, but the click of a bullet being loaded into a rifle was unmistakable. Castro shouted, "Shut up and listen" to the newcomer in Spanish, and I guess the person understood, since that was the last time I heard him raise his voice. After a short time, the American came out of the tent, went over to the car and had the driver open the trunk. The chauffer removed two heavy suitcases, placed them on the road and looked at the American for further instructions. In an imperious tone, one that you wouldn't even speak to a slave, the American shouted, "Pick them up and follow me."

The Cuban driver looked at us with downcast eyes. We were as embarrassed for him as he was, to be spoken to like that in front of other Cubans. Watching this melodrama unfold I'm sure he knew that we felt sorry for him and how he was addressed.

Lifting a suitcase in each hand he started to walk behind the American, when one of the valises fell from his grasp, hit the ground, and opened. The valise was crammed with high-denomination American dollars.

"Damn you, pick them up stupid, and stuff them into the valise," the American yelled.

The Cuban dropped to one knee and looked around, while we averted our eyes as if we didn't see the money or hear the insulting command and tone. He scooped the money into the valise, closed the latch, and followed the American into the tent. A few moments later, the driver came out and took his place behind the wheel of the automobile, followed shortly by the American. After the car left, one of the men who lived in this area before joining Castro said the American was the head of one of the largest American agricultural companies doing business on this part of the island.

That night with nothing to report on the radio, I stayed in my tent that was adjacent to the headquarter tent, listening to Fidel, Raul and Che laughing uproariously.

After sharing more than one bottle of rum, as could be seen by the bottles strewn on the ground, they were bragging about the "loan" they took from the "gringo" that was destined to go to Batista and now was theirs to buy more guns.

By this time seeing the inroads Castro was making, every American company was actively playing both ends against the middle, paying off both Batista and Castro so that whoever came out on top would be their ally. Castro was not stupid, and with all his rhetoric and declarations to the Cuban people, he was playing the same game with the world.

A week after the American's visit, the cane was ready for harvesting. Castro called me into his tent, "Rodriguez, I want you to see first-hand what I'm doing for the Cuban people against the American interests. Go with Ernesto and his group. When you come back to camp, I want you to broadcast what you saw but only in Spanish.

Be ready in ten minutes to join the squad.

I saluted," Si Commandante", retrieved a small writing pad and went to get ready.

It took about three hours to get down the hill and into the first fields of sugarcane.

We laughed, joked, and sang, there was no need for silence. In a day or so, the laborers will be in the fields doing the cutting. Ox drawn carts would carry the cut cane to the trains and from the trains to the factories to be pressed. Today the fields were ours to roam about as we wished.

As we crossed the first set of railroad tracks, Ernesto held up his hand for us to stop.

He reached into his backpack pulled out a hand grenade, walked over to a railroad track and wedged it alongside a rail. Tying a chord to the pin, he came back to where we were behind a wall. He pulled the chord, exploding the grenade, and destroying the rail. The trains on this track would not be moving anything. We did this on every set of tracks we came across completely cutting off the cane to the American processing factory. Then Ernesto cut a piece of cane, that was completely dry and highly inflammable, made it into a torch, lit it, and set fire to the grass to destroy the sugarcane fields. Within seconds the wind picked up the flame and in minutes the field was a mass of fast-spreading fire sending dark black smoke across the fields that in a few hours would cover the entire sky. To insure that there was no way to put the fire out, all the valves on the irrigation pumps were destroyed.

In four days the sugar cane, railroad tracks and factories in Oriente Province, plus four company towns were completely destroyed. The entire eastern part of Cuba was under acrid smoke and ash. By the end of the week all the Haitian and Jamaican cane cutters were sent back to their native lands. As Castro promised, his law prevailed. The fields were later cut up into small fincas (farms) and given to Cubans. American companies were completely out of business on the Eastern end of Cuba.

When we arrived back in camp Fidel, Raul and Che greeted us like prodigal sons. Guevara took me aside.

"Rodriguez- did you take notes?"

"Yes", I replied, "I have them right here if you want to read them."

"No, let's not waste time; you are immediately going to broadcast. Remember this will only broadcast in Spanish and only on Cuban frequencies. The time is not ripe for the gringos to know our plans, so for our American friends, we will say it was lightning strikes that caused the fires. For the present, anything we tell them will suffice since they are so gullible and cannot see, or don't want to see, the hand in front of their face. Better yet, let me have your notes and I'll write the script and do the broadcast. Wait for me in the radio tent."

An hour later Guevara walked in with a smug smile on his face.

"Do what you need to do, so I can get on the microphone."

The self-centered bastard never says please or thank you and at times, even though it would be certain death before a firing squad; I would like to punch him. Being an accredited doctor in Argentina, his birth country, didn't improve his personality any and to me he was one of the most obnoxious people I knew. At times, even Fidel and Raul were upset by his manner.

I handed him the microphone. He again asked me if it were only on Cuban frequencies. I nodded, and he began, "This is General Che Guevara of the Cuban Revolutionary Movement sending good news to the Cuban people. Our forces are marching westward and anticipate being in Havana by the end of this year. Batista and American companies are the first to feel the wrath of Fidel's forces. Let the Cuban people also know that these companies made overtures to pay off our beloved Fidel with the monies destined for Batista. Our response! Look to Cuba's eastern skies. The fires, the smoke, the ash is our response to all the American companies that are sucking the blood out of our Cuban people. Viva La Revolucion."

He turned around and handed the microphone back to me with a smirk on his face.

In all, I was with Fidel for close to a year. The only contact I had with him was when he or Guevara wanted to make a speech, asked me something about the radio, or when I needed a new part. I kept my thoughts to myself about his communistic leanings, hoping I was wrong, yet knowing my feelings were correct. My suspicions were being more solidified about Fidel and his real goals. The Russians seemed to be taking more than a passing interest in our Cuban revolution.

Messages going out and coming in on some frequencies were about Russian aid. I also overheard one where they would have emissaries in Havana when we arrived. It seemed strange that when a representative from the New York Times and Life Magazine interviewed Fidel, he kept assuring them that he had nothing to do with communism. He publicly separated himself from any Cuban communist movement or affiliation. I knew it was a lie, but maybe I thought that when we got to Havana things would sort themselves out.

January 1, 1959, we arrived in Havana! Batista is gone! Martial law has been declared. The casinos are closed and the gringos are gone but the streets are seeing a lot of blood. For some people it was the opportune time to get revenge on people that they perceived had done them wrong under Batista. Everyone close to Fidel, and Raul was jockeying for position and stepping over anyone to get into a position of power. The sound of gunfire from firing squads could be heard day and night. Fidel, while hailed as the Savior of Cuba, put Lleo in as President until such time as he would take over, and in my mind, another dictator was born.

Since radio transmissions were an integral part of Fidel's plan, in Havana, my small transmitting studio was directly across from his. Being so close I constantly saw Russians coming and going into his office, and the intuitions I had in the field about the movement drifting towards communism were proven correct. Castro was installing a communistic regime with him at the head, backed by Russia.

With all that was going on, I asked and was granted permission to go home on leave. It had been a year since I'd been home in Matanzas and months since I've seen or heard anything from my family.

Don started to thumb through the pages of his diary. I could see he stopped at a page that had Matanzas written across the top, "Have you ever had the experience of losing all your possessions?" he asked.

I turned off the recorder, looked at him, thought about it for a minute or so and said, "No. I've lost many things in my life, people, relationships, things, but never all at one time."

"You may recall the first night Jorge and I were reunited in Miami, we were sitting in a bar and Jorge was telling me what happened since I saw him last in Cuba. He told me about returning to his home in Matanzas after a year with Castro. Listen carefully to what I'm going to read. This is about a man who lost everything including his dreams. Please don't miss a word recording this."

CHAPTER 14

Jorge took a sip of his drink, rotated his neck a few times to relieve the tension in his muscles and continued, As the taxi was driving me up the long road to the hacienda, I was getting angrier and angrier with every passing mile. I couldn't believe it! Our plantation had been cut up into small (fincas) farms. Only a handful of people were working the land, and where people were congregated, rather than working the land, they were sitting on piles of rubble, smoking, and talking. Under Castro's directive, the granjeros (farmers) must have received their "fincas" but there seemed to be no organization, supervision, or purpose. Where once thousands of acres of well-maintained sugar cane and tobacco fields were, now seemed to be miniscule unkempt, unproductive farms with chickens running wild and vegetables gardens overgrown by weeds and trash.

The driver pulled up to the front door of the hacienda. I got out, paid him and he departed. The fountain in the circular driveway was lying in pieces around its pedestal. The flowerbeds my mother took so much pride in, now replaced by weeds. My home, the home built by strong arms and stronger backs generations ago now reduced to nothing but an old building in disrepair due to the hot sun and recent fierce storms from the ocean.

The overhang on the outdoor walkway was collapsing. The walk-way floor tile was partially torn up, with most tiles missing. The barrel red clay tile roof that withstood hurricanes for centuries had half its tiles lying on the ground. Every window had a broken glass. Apparently, there was no one here to care for the hacienda since it was taken over.

No one came out to greet me or to even see who was visiting. I walked to the entrance in anticipation of seeing Mamazita, Papa, or my sister. One heavy double oak door was partly opened on its ancient hinges, the other closed. I pushed the partly opened door to enter my home and it made the same squeaking noise I had heard since I was a baby. The house was completely bare. No rugs. No furniture. No drapes.

It was completely devoid of the feeling that anyone had ever lived there. Children of the squatters were running around playing games in the empty rooms that were littered with paper, empty cans and filth. I sat on the floor completely confused. Was this really my home? Slowly I got up and went through every room, and was overwhelmed by the condition I found throughout the hacienda. What happened, where is everyone? I was born in this home. I walked outside in disbelief to the rear of the house facing the ocean. A feeling of emptiness, a feeling of disbelief came over me. Facing me was an empty pedestal that once held a statue of a dolphin facing the Straits of Florida. I sat on the ground, too numb to feel anything and must have stared at the ocean for some time before realizing the sun was starting to set. A statement my father said came back to haunt me.

"En cada revolucion, los terratenientes y los educados son los primeros en ir ante un peloton de fusilamiento."

"In every revolution, the landowners and educators are the first to be put before a firing squad."

Not fully comprehending what I was experiencing, I walked the distance to our manager's house, hoping Jose was there and able to fill in some details of this nightmare. Jose had been with our family all his life, as was his father. I knocked and a voice told mc to come in. Jose was sitting in a chair facing the door when I opened it. He looked at me and started to cry, then got up, and put his arms around me.

"Jorgecito is it really you?"

He walked towards me with his arms outstretched as I did to him. We embraced as he sobbed, the tears running freely down his sun burnt copper cheeks.

"Jose, what happened?"

"Jorge" he said, holding his arms out to all points of the compass. They came one day, said people like your padre were against the Castro regime and took him to Havana. He's in jail, no one can see him. Your Madre is now living with her sister in Havana. Maria, I heard is now a doctor and is also living somewhere in Havana. They chopped up the plantation into little "fincas" saying that all the people have the right to Cuban land. The hacienda is now community property."

He poured rum from a bottle sitting on the table and handed me the tumbler, then poured himself one. I looked at my hand holding the glass and realized how badly it was trembling. It was as if I was watching someone with palsy. With all that happened that day I was exhausted physically and emotionally. I still could not comprehend all that was happening or what I saw. My mind could not absorb any more. I kept saying to myself that this was all a dream. I'll wake up soon. This cannot be happening. It cannot be!

I vaguely remember Jose asking me if I had anything to eat that day, insisting I have some beans that were on the stove and stay the night pointing to his own bed, saying he would sleep on the broken down couch in his one room wooden shack. With another glass of rum, I passed out but remembered Jose covering me when he put me to bed. I awakened the next morning to the crowing of a rooster, lying there as dawn came over the horizon, at first I didn't remember where I was. Then reality came drifting back. I needed to make plans. My first priority was to see my mother, if possible, get my father out of prison, and bring our family together again.

Jose shared his meager breakfast with me. When we finished he drove me to the railroad station in his car that was nearly as old as he was. Jose waited with me until the train pulled in. We embraced as old dear friends do, wished each other good luck and knew we would never see each other again.

As Jorge was telling me the story, I could feel the tension and anger building up within him. This Jorge sitting across from me was not the happy-go-lucky Jorge I knew.

Jorge was now a man driven by hate and the need for revenge.

Jorge looked at me.

"Don, my brother, wait till you hear the rest of this. I'm driven now and won't be happy until I can destroy as much of Castro and his people as I can. Rafael has introduced me to Cuban people here in Miami that have connections with your Government and the money and resources to overthrow Castro and give Cuba back to the people, I have joined them."

CHAPTER 15

"Jorge, how about something to eat", I asked, to relieve some of the tension.

"No Don, my story is nearing its' end. It feels good getting all this anger and frustration out of my system, just by telling it to you."

I heard the latch being jerked back. The door was thrown open and Aunt Clara was in my arms, tears falling down both our faces. Mamazita must have been in another room and had not heard her.

"Isabella! Isabella", she called my mother's name.

"Come quick, Jorge is here. Jorgecito is back."

Mamazita ran to join us and the three of us began hugging with tears of joy running down our cheeks. Being united lessened the sorrow of what had happened in our lives over the past year. We moved into the house and closed the door against the prying eyes of the street captains, who reported everything and anyone immediately to the authorities that seemed unusual or didn't belong in the neighborhood.

We no sooner sat down when Aunt Clara excused herself to go into the kitchen to make something for me to eat. Mamazita; poor, tired Mamazita, couldn't stop crying or holding my hand, or looking at me, touching me, as if I would disappear in the next moment. Her luxurious black hair was now streaked with gray and her dress fit as if it were made for someone much heavier. Looking at her, I realized she had aged tremendously since I saw her last. Then she started to narrate what happened in Mantanzas, what happened to Papa, and why she was staying with Aunt Clara. While she was speaking I really looked at her. Hair mostly gray, her eyes surrounded by black rings from lack of sleep, lines of worry on her forehead, God knows what she must be going through especially now with Papa being in prison. My mind opened to the fate that Papa must be enduring. I pushed the thought of him being dead immediately from my mind.

She looked at me, stopped and said, " I'll tell you more after you eat and rest, then tell me everything that's happened to my Jorgecito this past year."

Just then Aunt Clara brought in a plate of arroz con pollo (chicken and rice) and a glass of wine, saying, "Jorgecito, you look like a skeleton. Eat first and we'll talk later."

I had so much to talk about. I talked while I ate. For the next few hours, I gave them a synopsis of what happened since I left the plantation after Papa's birthday party. My eyes started to close and I felt I was nodding off. After a short time, I started to have difficulty putting a coherent sentence together. Apologizing to Mamazita and Aunt Clara, I asked, "Aunt Clara may I use the shower and maybe lie down for an hour or so?"

I had not had a shower or shaved in hot water for a year and need to wash my body and mind clean of everything I saw and did.

"Of course, Jorgecito, and while you're taking a shower let me see what clothes your cousin Leo left before immigrating to Miami."

What a the blessing hot water was, especially with the scent and feel of a bar of soap, a sharp razor, shaving cream and clean towels. I forgot what it felt like after all these months living in the bush, washing in a cold running stream and shaving when I could with a dull razor. I was feeling human once again. I lay down on Leo's bed, giving a blessing for a soft mattress and clean sheets.

After nearly a year, I felt warm, clean and secure. I remember closing my eyes and slept like a baby until the sun shining in the window awakened me. Rested and wearing my cousin's clothes, I walked downstairs and was ready to hear the story of what happened after I left the plantation. I kissed and said good morning to Aunt Clara who was busy making breakfast. I walked into the breakfast area to kiss Mama and stopped short. She was feeding an infant in a high chair. Mama looked at me with a big smile on her face, her eyes reflecting the love she had for the child.

"Jorge, meet your nephew, Eduardo."

"Eduardo! Whose child is this?"

"This child is from the love of Maria and Don, my first grandchild."

"Does Don know?"

"No! How could he? At first, Maria did not want to burden Don since he was under so much stress starting his new business. Then a few months later, when she was sure she was pregnant, all lines of communication with the States were cut. There was no way of contacting him to let him know. Aunt Clara and I helped her through the pregnancy so that she could finish her education. Eduardito is healthy, well fed as you can see, and is living in a loving environment with us as is Maria."

When I looked at the little boy, there was a definite resemblance to Don, especially the blonde hair and blue eyes, a cute, chubby little boy. I turned to Mama, "So Mamazita, now tell me what happened after I left?"

Mama's hands were nervously twisting a napkin as she started.

"Shortly after Christmas Castro's soldiers came through Matanzas they stopped at the plantation. Being young men and Cubans, we fed them and gave them shelter for a few days as if they were our own sons. A week after the soldiers left, another group of about ten men came, saying they represented the new Cuban government. They read some statement that all land belonged to Cuba and, under the direction of Castro, seized the hacienda, as well as the plantation. We told them that it had been in our family for generations but they did not want to hear it. They gave us until noon the next day to leave everything and go, or we would be forcibly thrown out. We were only allowed to take a suitcase each. Papa told them that you were with Castro, but that did not do any good either. He started arguing with them, and in a rage raised his fist as if to hit one. They beat him up. They beat up an old man and told him if he did not quiet down, they would shoot him in front of his wife. What were we to do! The next morning we packed our luggage like beggars and came to Clara's house. Fortunately, we had time to telephone Maria at school, to tell her where we would be. Papa, being very angry went to see someone in Havana, and we have not seen or heard from him since. We heard he is in prison but where in Havana, we have no idea. No one, even old friends, is willing to help us for fear of becoming involved and the same thing happening to them."

When she finished telling me about what happened at the hacienda, tears started to fall from her eyes. She had suffered enough grief and looked much older than she was. I didn't have the heart to tell her I was there, and what a deplorable state I found it in. Better to leave the past and live in the future, but I could feel the anger welling up inside me for not only my family but also the lies and injustice that we were again letting rule us. That is all Cuba needed- another dictator whose' string is being pulled by another foreign power.

"How about Maria?" I interrupted.

"She is now living in Havana, she must know people with influence at the University or the hospital. Have you spoken to her?" I asked.

"We have and she's trying but everything is upside down. There is no authority, no department to go to, and no head of anything. Castro has taken over everything no matter how minute it is. His decisions are the only decisions. We were told that the only other persons that can do anything are his brother Raul or someone named Che Guevara, but getting to either of them is as difficult as getting to Castro.

About a month ago when Maria came home she said that she was selected by someone to be on posters throughout Cuba saying that she's the model for the New Cuban Woman, but even if this is so, she can't seem to help."

I finished eating and said, "Look, its early where can I find Maria? I want to speak to her and see what's going on and maybe how I can help."

Mama gave me the address of the pediatric hospital where Maria was training, which was only a short walk from Aunt Clara's house.

While walking to the hospital I could see and feel the tension, fear, and suspicion on the people's faces as I passed them on the streets. Where the streets of Havana always resounded with music and laughter even under the gringos, these same streets were now somber and silent under Castro. No one passing me raised their eyes from the sidewalk or said "hello".

At the hospital's reception desk, I asked for Maria Rodriguez. How strange those words sounded; my little sister, close to being a doctor and a mother.

"Is she expecting you, Senor? She's very busy and unless you have an appointment, it's impossible to see her on so little notice."

"No, I have no appointment but I'm sure it's all right. I'm her brother."

Thinking it would add weight I added, "And tell her I just arrived with Fidel in Havana and its most important I see her immediately."

The receptionist immediately lifted the phone at the sound of Castro's name and paged Maria. If the truth be known, hearing my sister being paged, gave me a feeling of pride.

In a few minutes, a woman in a white lab coat, with a stethoscope hanging around her neck came down the hallway.

"Jorgecito, is it really you?"

"Is this Dr. Rodriquez really my baby sister?"

We hugged, and she led me into a small room off the hallway.

"Tell me how you are", she said.

I held up my hand to silence her, "Let's not talk about me. First, let me congratulate you on being a mother, I saw the little boy this morning, but more important what has happened to Papa?

How do we find out what prison he is in, if he has been injured or if he is dead. How could we get him out? Who do you know?"

As I blurted the words, I knew the tone was angry and the words accusing but once out I couldn't retract them. She looked at me.

"I'm trying Jorge, honestly I am, but there's an entirely new wind blowing over Cuba and part of it is sweeping away the old nobility.

"What nobility!" I shouted. "We're talking about our father."

"Jorge, I'm trying but it will take time."

"I can't believe this. You're here as a doctor because of the education your parents gave you. You didn't do this by yourself; you owe your parents something for this."

(I extended my hand to the room).

"I can't get through to you. You must know someone. Aunt Clara mentioned that you are doing very well and may be running this entire pediatric hospital in a few years, so you must have some influence."

"There is no time," I shouted. "You can hear the firing squads by just opening any window in Havana. You must know somebody who can get him released, if he is still alive".

"Jorge, calm down and for heaven's sake, lower your voice."

I looked at her, full of anger and frustration as I realized what happened to our family was a small indication of what was happening all over Cuba. The anger wasn't directed at Maria, but our new regime and I couldn't direct it elsewhere. With all the rage in my heart I stupidly said, "You're not my sister!" I turned my back on her, slammed the door and left the hospital as fast as I could.

I felt I had to do something, even if it meant going directly to Castro. All I wanted to do was lash out and hurt someone.

CHAPTER 16

I was so absorbed in Jorge's story that I did not notice the number of people that were filling up the restaurant. I looked at my watch. It was dinnertime and we have already been here over four hours. I held up my hand.

"Jorge it's dinner time. Let's take a break and get some dinner. Do you need to call someone?"

"My god! I didn't realize I had been talking for that long. I was supposed to have a dinner date tonight with my girlfriend."

"Amigo, you've only been in Miami a short time and you already have a girlfriend?" I kiddingly asked.

"It's an old friend," Jorge said". I casually knew Gloria and her husband when I as in the Cuban Air Force. The poor guy died in a plane crash soon after their baby was born. Her family moved to Miami a year ago, and so did she. We kept in touch and when I came to Miami, we renewed our friendship and started dating."

"Is it serious amigo?"

"Si, we're talking of marriage."

Jorge got up to make his phone call. When he returned, he had a big grin on his face. "Don, she's wonderful, you have to meet her. Now, let's eat."

After dinner, he continued, "It was only a ten minute walk to the Capitol building, where Fidel, Raul and Guevara had installed themselves as well as their cohorts as the heads of Government. The streets were lined with people standing around with no purpose and since a month had passed since Castro is taking over, the only words to describe Havana and the people were "dirty and depressing". Batista was gone and a new life was supposed to be dawning. Castro was supposed to make everything right."

The steps leading up to the Capitol building were nothing like they were under Batista. Previously, they were washed and swept twice a day, now they were a disgrace.

Old newspapers, sandwich wrappers, liquor bottles, empty soda, and beer cans were strewn over the streets and Capitol steps. People were sleeping or passed out on the marble steps so that anyone going into or coming out of the building had to step over or around their bodies. This was our Capitol... this was the heart of Cuba. Inside the building was no better, only here people were running around like ants, clutching papers and shouting. It could only be described as chaos within chaos. It bothered me because the Cuban people had always taken pride in their surroundings. For now though, I had a mission and the condition of the area was not my concern.

It may be asked why Fidel let things disintegrate as he did. My answer is that he was swept into Havana on a tide of propaganda and hero worship. There was absolutely no infrastructure to back up any plans he may have had, nor did he make any effort to continue the government offices as they were under Batista. Revenge and the firing squad were the only two things he was interested in. Social services could wait.

Getting to Fidel was impossible. I had a feeling that was going to happen before I even started, but I had to do something. I stepped into an alcove to think if there was anyone I knew who possibly had the political power to help me. Then, like a light bulb turning on, it came. It was none other than the man closest to Castro, the man who wrote the lies I used to spout over the airwaves, the man who laughed at putting people to death, but was afraid for his own life, none other than the good Argentine doctor turned communist, Che Guevara.

His office was on the main floor in an obscure corridor. I opened the door and his assistant, Hector, whom I knew quite well, informed me that Guevara wasn't in. Hector and I had shared many a meal, cigar, rum and laughs over the past year while in the field. It was a camaraderie shared by all soldiers, but between Hector and me, a real friendship.

"Jorge, I thought you were stationed with your troops outside of town, not with the select few assigned here", he said with a smile.

"I'm not assigned here; I just need to see Guevara."

"About what? Maybe I can help." "Hector, I have a personal problem and need to speak with him. Have you any idea when Guevara will return?"

"I have no idea, or even if he'll be back today. He doesn't tell me his schedule. Can I help you? Think before you answer, it may cost you a dinner."

"Hector this is serious. My papa is in prison. He's an old man who got angry, and because he lifted his hand to one of the agents that were forcing him and my mother to leave our home, they beat him up and threw him in jail. No one can get to see him and we don't know if he's even alive."

"This is really serious my friend. What can I do to help?"

"You can relate this to Guevara and tell him I'm begging him in the name of our working relationship these past months, to find out how my father is and get me in to see him."

"Seguro, (sure) and where can he reach you?"

"I'll be at this telephone number. It's my Aunt's house where I am having dinner. Then after 10 tonight, I'll be back at the radio station where Fidel made his speech today and I'll be there all day tomorrow."

We shook hands, Hector saying, as a friend he would do his best to pass the information along to Guevara. I stayed a few moments longer to pass the time and then left.

I went back to my Aunt's house, told them what had transpired, and while nothing was certain, it gave us a little hope. We had dinner together, I played with little Eduardo and it came to me that I never asked Aunt Clara how her son was doing in the States.

"Aunt Clara, in all this time I never asked you how my cousin Leo is doing."

She looked at me as any proud mother would and said, "He's doing well. He met an American girl at the University of Miami. Her father is in construction and Leo is working for him learning the trade. He wrote that his plans were for them to get married in June in Miami, and then get married again here in Havana, so the Cuban family could be part of it. However that's out of the question since under the new laws not anyone who left Cuba can return. Fidel calls them "worms". Too bad his father, Enrico, isn't alive to see his son getting married but now neither can I. Leo wanted me to move to the United States after his Miami wedding, but I told him that at my age with all the family here, I'd rather stay in a place I know with people I know, and wouldn't know how to make new friends." She sighed deeply, "Now even leaving Cuba is impossible."

After dinner I changed into a clean uniform my mother had washed and ironed, thanked my aunt for taking care of my mother, and kissed them both goodbye. To say goodbye to Eduardito, I went to the high chair and let him wrap his little fat fingers around one of my fingers. More important for them and me, being stationed only a few miles from Aunt's Clara's house, I could spend time with them and help where and how I could. At least it would give us all some semblance of family again.

At the radio station there was a written message waiting for me. Guevera couldn't do anything since Papa was one of the landowners that put Cuba in the position it was.

This was followed by the same written diatribe by Fidel of giving the country back to its rightful owners, the Cuban people, not the wealthy land barons, the same communist line I had spouted from a script into a microphone hundreds of times for Guevara and Fidel. He thanked me in the name of the Cuban revolution, and while not releasing me from the armed forces, transferred me to the Agricultural Department where there was an opening flying crop dusting aircraft in the Matanzas area, ending his message with, "Cubans need food."

The sadistic bastard always got his pound of flesh by rubbing salt in the wounds! Now he graciously gave me the opportunity to see what my family's plantation looked like every day from the air. My only thought was to one day have the opportunity to wrap my hands around Guevara's throat. Papa had been so right, and I, so wrong.

That night, disheartened and very angry, I went back to my Aunt's house and explained to Mama and Aunt what had happened and how I couldn't find out anything about Papa or what his physical health was. The faint glimmer of hope was again replaced by gloom.

Mamazita, Aunt Clara and I sat around making small talk and were ready to go to bed when the doorbell rang. I looked at my watch. It was 10 p.m., we looked at each other.

At that hour of the night under Batista and now Castro, if someone wanted to visit, they would always telephone first. With only a knock on the door, we immediately anticipated something bad. Aunt Clara and Mama started to tremble since Maria doesn't come home from the hospital until after midnight. With one hand, Aunt Clara pointed to the door, and then me wanting me to open the door. My anger from this afternoon had not abated and my only wish was that I had a gun in my hand to get even for what they did to Papa and the insult from Guevara.

With that thought in my head I walked to the door, opened the peephole and looked out on Maria's face. Without saying a word, I swung the door wide, turned my back on her and walked back into the room where Mama and Aunt Clara were.

"Buenos noches Mamazita, Aunt Clara and even you Jorge. I got off early and forgot my key," she said, as she laid two large bags of groceries down on the kitchen table. She came back into the living room, and kissed Eduardo who was sound asleep in the crib they had for him in the living room.

"I see my brother is still in a foul mood about Papa being in prison, or am I the cause of his bad mood, or perhaps Fidel is. Or is he upset about getting a job flying in Matanzas?" She looked at me and said, "Yes, I know all about it".

"Let me tell you something, dear brother. While you were playing soldier for a year, it was I who kept the family in food and other necessities, not you. It was I, both under Batista and Castro who kept what is left of our family safe here at Aunt Clara's, not you. I do have contacts, and these contacts are what are keeping us safe and well fed in these changing times. I will tell you something else. I have worked too hard and too long to have you charging around like a bull in a china shop, jeopardizing my position and reputation. Castro may be a communist; I do not really care if he is red, green, white or blue. All I care about is taking care of the babies that are sick, and need care. I am completely dedicated to my profession and have no interest in politics or who is running Cuba. If Castro is instituting national health care and helping sick children and I can do my bit, I'm all for it."

I went over to her, apologized for the way I acted and sat silent while she spent time gossiping with Mamazita and Aunt Clara until they excused themselves and went to bed, leaving Maria and me alone.

"Well," said Maria, "now that we are alone, tell me what you have been doing with yourself, by the way you've lost a lot of weight and look terrible."

"Are you asking me as a doctor or my sister?" I joked.

We looked at each other, smiled, and the warm feeling of being a loving brother and sister flowed through each of us again. We were so different but yet so similar.

I started to tell her a bit, then realized, why? It's was all ancient history now.

I knew what I had to do, and talking politics or venting my feelings would do no one any good. In fact it could very well come back to later bite me. Maria told me how difficult medical school was and how busy she was now. Then out of the clear blue sky said, "I saw Don a few times."

"Where, when?"

"Just before Castro closed down travelling out of the Country, Don came to Havana at Christmas to see me. We stayed here for a few nights in Aunt Clara's house and soon after he left, I found out I was pregnant. Jorge, I miss him so much. He left the import-export company in New York, started his own business and as far as I last heard, was doing very well. He always asked about you and Rafael and gave me his telephone number. In case I ever saw either of you, he wanted you to have it. I think it's in my purse, let me look."

For the few seconds Maria looked through her purse, a million happy moments flashed through my mind of the three of us on weekends, when Maria was going to University. Were we ever so young, so innocent, never thinking that life changes or that life would not always be fun and games. What a rude awakening. Maria reached out her hand with the telephone numbers on it. "Here they are. I have copies all over, even at work. I can't wait till we're all together again and if you ever reach him, tell him I love him and we have a beautiful son."

After breakfast the next morning, Maria and I hugged and looked into each other's face, both our eyes were moist. Maria, kissed me on the cheek again, and said, "I accept your apology of last night. Do anything you feel you need to do and if it means leaving Cuba, I'm sure the family will understand. Just be careful, little Eduardo needs an uncle."

We went our separate ways; Maria back to the hospital and I to hitch a ride to Matanzas to see about my new job. Wearing a uniform, with most of the highway traffic being military vehicles, I was in Matanzas within a few hours. I had lived there all my life and with the directions given me, I knew exactly where to look for a small landing strip.

CHAPTER 17

I was standing on a knoll looking down at a dirt runway where three biplanes, built before the Second World War, were tied down. There were no hangers, just a small building that may serve as the office. All repairs and loading of the planes must be done outdoors since I saw no facilities for that purpose. Since speculation was useless, I started down the hill and stopped at the first plane, a bright yellow painted Stearman biplane that American Navy pilots trained in, in the early 40's, and called them "Yellow Perils". I guess after the war, your government gave some of these planes to Batista. In my early teens, a friend's father, who flew in the Second World War, bought one of these aircraft privately, at an American government surplus sale, and flew it to Cuba. While my friend and I were too young to get a pilot's license, he taught us to fly and when he thought we were competent enough, let us solo. By the time we reached the age of eighteen, we both qualified for our pilot's license.

There were no military markings on this plane and as I walked slowly around it, caressing it with the palm of my hand, my eyes fondly took it all in and for a few moments, a feeling of nostalgia swept over me of a time long ago of innocents. The canvas covering on the wings and fuselage felt tight, the struts between the wings seemed solid. I was shocked to find a handle for the aircrafts inertia starter lying on the ground, under the propeller. The same type handles that were used to start the cars by cranking in the 1920 and 30s. I had not flown a plane like this in years. In fact, I did not think they were any still in use, airworthy or presently flying.

"Do you remember that plane Don?" Jorge asked.

I smiled and nodded my head and responded, "I recall a mechanic standing on the right wing root cranking the starter and when it was spinning he would yell "clear", then after you shouted, "clear", he'd yell, "contact" and your response would be lost as you engaged the propeller."

"Strange, we used the same words in English here in Cuba, "clear" and "contact".

Being close to this plane was like going back in time with an old friend. I climbed onto the wing to look into the cockpit when I heard a door slam and a person yelling, "Get down from there!"

I turned around and facing me was a man with a pistol in his hand. Climbing down I walked over to him with my arms in the air.

"Who are you?" he asked.

"I'm the new pilot. I wanted to look the plane over, before reporting to"el jefe"

(The Chief). My name is Jorge Rodriguez, what's yours?" I asked, as I reached out to shake his hand.

He lowered the gun, extended his hand and at the same time said, "My name's Sako, I'm the one and only mechanic. Let's go into the office and I'll introduce you to "El Jefe."

He opened the door of the office and sitting at a desk was an older man with cheeks reddened and weathered by years of sitting in an open cockpit.

"Are you the new pilot they sent us from Havana?" he asked.

"Si, my name is Jorge Rodriguez," I said shaking his hand.

"Bien," Call me Toni. I am in charge of this operation. Say, are you the Rodriguez that owned that big plantation a few miles west of here?"

My mind spun, what do I do? Lic or say yes?

After a few seconds of hesitation, I replied, "Yes, the plantation was ours."

"You were a captain in the Cuban Air Force, no?"

"Si, I was, but some time ago."

"Ever fly one of those beasts sitting out there?" he said, as he pointed to the biplanes.

"A hundred years ago," I responded smiling.

"Well, the front seat is taken up with spray equipment, so you can't get any dual instruction, but let me give you a rundown on what I think you need to know, and then you can take it up for a spin. With the hours you've flown, you should get the feel of the plane in an hour. Just remember on landing this has a tail-skid and you haven't the control you would have as on a modern plane's tricycle gear."

After giving me a briefing, I asked, "How many other pilots are there, Toni?"

"You, me and one other. Listen my friend; I'm in charge, but the other pilot is politically connected and reports directly to Havana, so to prevent any grief, listen to what he says, do what he says, and keep your thoughts to yourself."

"When do I start?"

"Take a bicycle from the office and find a place to sleep in one of the nearby villages. You start flying tomorrow, and we'll start dropping insecticides for mosquito control the day after. The plane will handle differently with insecticides in the tanks because of the additional weight. The most important things are to keep one eye on your air speed and the other on how close you are to the ground, especially in steep turns. That is when pilots get killed, usually when the plane is loaded and stalls out."

I went into town and, with the economy as bad as it was, and easily found a furnished room to rent by the week in what was once a fashionable small hotel, but now housed itinerant government workers. An elderly woman who had no family ran it and was happy to have someone fill the vacancy. The room was sparsely furnished, but most importantly, the bed was clean, and the towels fresh. Not knowing what the future held, I wanted to be as free of any possessions as possible and this room fit my plans perfectly.

The next day when I reported, I met the third pilot. We disliked each other immediately. He had an attitude of superiority and assumed a role of authority over me. He made no bones about being pro-Castro. He took it upon himself to have me stand at military attention while he read me the dos and don'ts of what he expected and I laughed to myself, anticipating him wanting me to salute him when he finished his speech.

What concerned me most was the document I had to sign, namely:

1. Fuel was by the mission. There was to be no extra fuel in the tanks at any time.
2. Never get closer than 5 miles to the Straits of Florida.
3. Never land anywhere other than where we took off except in an emergency.
4. Never have anyone in the plane with you.

Penalty for infractions of these rules was imprisonment and possible death.

I signed the contract.

I took off on my first flight. The wheels rumbled on the dirt runway as I advanced the throttle. Small stones thrown up by the propeller hit the underside of the plane, then smoothed out as I reached airspeed. As I slowly brought the joystick back, the plane left the earth and for the first time in a year, I felt free. If you never piloted a plane solo it is impossible to describe the feeling of not being earthbound, nor can one imagine it. You're with the gods playing with the clouds, climbing up one side and coasting down the other. You have the ability in your hands to forget gravity, traffic on roads, other people, and politics. You can dive towards the earth, climb to the heavens, turn upside down, or roll to your heart's content. You are a child again. You're free! Truly free!

I did a few touch and go landings and on the last, looked to the west where our plantation was, and north over the Straits of

Florida towards Key West where freedom waited over the horizon. The plan that had lain dormant in my mind for so long, solidified and at that instant I knew exactly what I was going to do and how I was going to do it. The only thing was, I didn't know when.

The months passed rapidly. I managed to see Mamazita, Aunt Clara, and Maria every few weeks. Mama and Aunt Clara were fine, Maria and the baby were also doing well and most importantly, from what Maria was told, Papa was being released from prison shortly.

The flying was fun and I was being teased for carrying a glass jar in the cockpit, telling everyone I had weak kidneys. In reality, I was siphoning a small amount of gas from the trucks and farm equipment and dumping it into a five gallon container I had buried in the fields in back of the office, where few people ever went. The glass jar in the cockpit was the same type I was using to siphon gas. If anyone saw me carrying a glass jar, they wouldn't think anything of it. The octane was lower than aviation fuel and it would eventually ruin the engine by making it run hot and rough, but it was the only option left if I was to get out of Cuba. Russians were becoming more noticeable in the cities. Their equipment, including aircraft, were arriving by shipload every day and Fidel was more openly spouting communist doctrines. Every time I visited the family, I hinted at my intentions of flying out of Cuba. If I didn't show up for a time, I'm sure they would have guessed where I was, but the longer I procrastinated, the more difficult leaving would become. Time to make my move was running out.

One Sunday, late afternoon, when I knew no one would be around I bicycled to the landing strip. It was deserted, just as I had anticipated it would be, with not even a guard. Either everyone was with their family, partying, listening to a soccer match on the radio or grouped around a bar's TV set in town.

Circumstances allowed for a change in plans. My cache of fuel hidden in the ground was no longer needed with a gas truck at my disposal. I forced open the gas trucks door with a screwdriver, jumped the ignition wires, started the engine and backed the truck up to a plane. Once in position with the fuel hose inserted into the planes tank, I pressed the electric button to start pumping gas through the line, climbed on the plane and pressed the gas nozzle. All the fuel I need started flowing into the plane's tank.

I was now totally committed! This was my chance.

My nerves were on edge. The gas seemed to be only dripping from the hose into the fuel tank, and after what seemed an eternity I hoped I had enough fuel to get me to Florida. I put the hose back on its rack on the truck, and backed the truck away from the plane to clear the wings. My only thought was that if I'm caught now, I'm dead.

Constantly looking around, I had yet to see anyone. I left the wood wheel chocks under the front of the plane's wheels so the plane wouldn't move when the propeller started to spin, stood on the wing and started to crank the starter by hand. When it was spinning at maximum speed, I climbed into the cockpit, stood on the brakes and gave it full throttle. With the plane shuddering from the strain it was under I released the brakes. The wheels jumped over the chocks and I took off straight ahead without looking at the windsock to see which direction the wind was coming from. As soon as I was airborne, I banked to what I hoped was an approximate a heading of 000 degrees, due north. I had no charts, only an uncorrected compass, but at that heading at about 3,000 feet I should be able to spot some part of the Keys or Dry Tortugas within an hour. Once airborne I kept the plane no higher than one hundred feet, and once over the ocean, as close to the surface as possible to evade Cuban radar or any Cuban or Russian fighters patrolling Cuban air space.

Scared? I was petrified. From nerves, sweat was pouring down my face, my shirt was sticking to me, my heart was pumping as if I were running from death itself. With no goggles, my eyes were slits to keep them from tearing in the slipstream. I kept turning my head, looking behind me, above me, both sides of me on the lookout for Cuban fighters. The Cuban Air Force was now using Russian aircraft and there was word that Russian pilots were also flying some of these plancs. Without question any plane flying towards the States would be shot down immediately and in this old biplane with its maximum speed of 110 mph, they need not shoot it down. Simply passing close at supersonic speed would tear the plane apart. I checked my watch; it was exactly 14:38.

I was in the air only five minutes but it already seemed like hours. After twenty minutes, I thought I was far enough off the Cuban Coast and in International waters to climb a few thousand feet, making it easier for American radar to pick me up. My altimeter just touched 1,700 feet, when two American military aircraft pulled alongside, one on each side, they appeared out of nowhere. Both pilots motioned to me in the direction of Key West. I waved back and thankfully gave them a thumbs up with my free hand. One locked himself off my right wing while the second plane pulled in front of me to lead me down to the airport. I made it! I was free! I was exhausted. Only when the plane rolled to a stop did I realize I never fastened my seat belt.

The Navy, U.S. Immigration and two intelligence groups, immediately questioned me. The only thing on my mind was perhaps later they would allow me to call you at the telephone numbers Maria had given me, and here I am.

Incredible! By this time the restaurant was devoid of all its customers. The kitchen helpers were starting to mop the floors and clear off the tables. Even the fellow behind the bar was gone. We had been sitting here over seven hours.

"Jorge, you must be exhausted, it's 3 a.m. John and I have a meeting this morning at 09:00 to go over some plans about Cuba. Let's get a taxi, I'll drop you off wherever you're staying and I'll head back to the hotel. I'll see you and Rafael at 8 a.m., Monday at Chalks."

We took a taxi and a short time later, it stopped in front of an apartment building in South Miami. Jorge and I got out and we embraced. No words other than "see you Monday", were said, but the emotion was felt by both of us. A half hour later, I was back in my room thinking of Maria and my son. Sleep did not come that night but a million questions did, along with the guilt of not being with her during her pregnancy, not being with her when she gave birth, or again thinking, did I do right by leaving Cuba.

That morning I met with John in the dining room and over breakfast our conversation drifted over a myriad of topics such as Cuba, my business, governments, money, power and how it all affected people's lives one way or the other. Breakfast completed, we shook hands, I again thanked him for bringing me to Miami to be with Jorge and Rafael, said goodbye and told him I would see him Monday at eight, at Chalks. As he turned to leave, John smiled and said, "See you later Dad", he knew I was a father before I did.

CHAPTER 18

Monday morning at the arranged time, John, Jorge, Rafael, and I gathered at Chalks where we boarded a twin engine, amphibian aircraft, taxied down the ramp into Biscayne Bay and, on takeoff, passed four luxury cruise ships tied to their dock in Port Miami. Less than an hour later, we landed in Key West, and our training began.

The public marina had every type of power or sailboat of every size and description. Outboard engines, inboard engines, inboard-outboard engines, gas, diesels, single screw, twin screw, you name it, it was there. John led us down one of the piers, and stopped at the stern of a 45-foot sport fishing boat with a flying bridge named the "Nina".

"O.K. guys, this is all yours so let's climb on board, and talk."

We hauled in the stern lines, pulled the boat to the dock, jumped onto the transom, then down to the deck, and proceeded into the cabin. As we sat down, John started to speak, "Your job for the next few weeks is simple," said John. "All you have to do is take the boat out, keep it 12 miles off Cuba for a few hours and come back.

What we are accomplishing is seeing how tight their Coast Guard and Air Force is and how forceful they are in maintaining the 12 mile limit."

"And what if we're shot at?" I asked.

"Turn and run," he said, "and if they persist, call Key West for military aircraft response."

"Do we have weapons on board?" Jorge asked.

"Negative, this is only a fishing boat," was his reply.

"One question," asked Rafael. "What about any refugees in boats or rafts we come across?"

"Pick them up, sink their rafts and if their boats are big enough, or sea worthy enough, tow them back in. If not, sink them."

"Look John," I asked, "What's the overall picture? What is the ultimate reason for doing this? The government isn't spending all this money for us to enjoy the sea air?"

"Honestly I don't know, but it's my guess that it has something to do with what's happening in the Everglades over near Naples, Florida," was his response.

What was happening in the Florida Everglades, Guatemala, and Nicaragua were no State secret. The American Government was training Cuban refugees for a possible return to Cuba. It was in all the newspapers and everyone even remotely connected to the Cuban population or read the South Florida newspapers knew about it, as did Fidel.

The boat was assigned a sector east of Havana and we treated it like a mini-vacation, with all expenses paid by Uncle Sam. Once in a great while a Cuban military plane would circle us then fly off. Only once did we see a Cuban patrol boat and that stayed well within the Cuban twelve-mile International limit. We did pick up a few dehydrated people and sunk a few makeshift boats and rafts, but they were few since the Gulf Stream moving East swept them out of our sector. In Cuba, people were forming lines at every foreign embassy in Havana applying for visas to get to any country, but with Fidel closing that door, the only alternative was to take to the sea. The trickle of boat people soon became a river of humanity. Anything that could float started to fill the Straits between Cuba and the United States; canoes, rowboats, log rafts, empty oil drums lashed together, even empty plastic containers held together with adhesive tape. Anything and everything that could float was used. Some people were rescued, most drowned, some were caught and shot. The fortunate Cubans, who left before Castro took over, the people that had the foresight to take their assets with them to Miami, now had boats that they, at their own expense, took to the ocean rescuing these people struggling to get the States. The Cubans who had planes, also at their own expense, would take to the air, and by radio direct the rescue boats to where their fellow Cubans could be found and picked up. In the United States, a law was passed; any Cuban landing on American soil would be given asylum.

One day at high noon, with the sun at its brightest, the seas glassy smooth and the reflected sunlight off the surface so bright you needed sunglasses, Jorge thought he saw something in the water. He was about 25 feet above the deck in a shaded tuna platform, and had better visibility than we did. He called down and said that there was an object about 200 feet ahead, at about ten degrees off our port bow. At the time, Rafael was at the helm and I was in the cabin monitoring a radio frequency used in ship-to-ship chatter. Rafael swung the wheel over, cut the throttles and we slowly drifted to where this object was.

All we could see were four heads above the water. Getting closer we saw they were sitting in a very large inner tube that had lost most of its air, with the top of the tube level with the surface of the ocean. Pulling alongside, I took a gaff and pulled the tube to the boat. In it were a man, a woman, and two children, all tied to the tube so they couldn't fall overboard, all dead. Hanging from the tube was what looked like an iron gate that served as a floor and a makeshift mast lashed in an upright position for a sail. Remnants of a cloth sail still fluttered from it. God only knows how long they were drifting, or how desperate they must have been to leave Cuba as a family, as they had. With the water sloshing in and out of the tube, crabs and fish have been nibbling at their bodies for some time. From the neck down, they were almost skeletons. From the neck up their faces were the color of dark leather from the sun.

I had Rafael and Jorge unshackle the 40-pound Danforth anchor from the anchor chain at the bow and slowly lowered it into the center of the tube. I tied my bowie knife to the gaff, punched holes in the tube to release all the air, and Rafael said a prayer in Spanish as the weight of the anchor caused the tube to slowly sink. We couldn't help looking at the poor souls, thinking our own thoughts, until the inner tube and its cargo went under. I started the engines, we did not look back.

People were desperate to leave Cuba by any means, but they did not realize that while the distance between Cuba and Florida is only ninety miles, with the currents and severe tropical storms that can come up out of nowhere, a flat sea can change to a twenty foot raging ocean in minutes. I wondered if this was ever included in their decision making, or was the desperation so intense that this danger was never fitted into the equation for survival.

Most days were spent enjoying the sunshine, dozing off to the gentle rocking of the boat and writing a humorous report on the day's activities to be left at the dock master for John to pick up. But all good things must come to an end and as we tied up one evening John was waiting for us, and we instinctively knew the vacation was over.

John hopped aboard and said, "Sorry fellas, the party's over. Let's go into the cabin. It's cozy without prying eyes and ears around."

"You guys have done a great job", he said. "I shared all the information you gave me with the group I am working with. They need time to analyze it and tie it together with the rest of the sectors to get the overall pictures of what we are up against and what the next step in the plan should be. Take the rest of the week off, and we'll get together Monday morning.

During our break from work, our nights were usually spent finding new places to have dinner, having a few beers, watching the sunset or just engaging in men's talk while sitting on the boat. With the number of Cuban refugees now living there and more arriving every day, it was no secret that Castro was infiltrating some of his own personnel with them. We made it a policy never to ever talk about boats or politics whenever we were around other people in the event someone picked up a clue as to what we were doing or about to do.

On the weekend, Jorge and Rafael went back to Miami to be with their families. I found some excuse not to join them, knowing the possibility of what the future could hold, I did not want to get too emotionally close to their families. Being this close to Jorge and Rafael was enough. I had already learned how difficult separation could be in my relationship with Maria.

My weekend was spent renting a car and visiting places I had never been to before in Florida while I was stationed there years before, while in the Navy.

Monday came; we were all on the, "Nina" having coffee, when John jumped aboard. We followed him into the cabin, sat down, and waited for him to speak.

"As of next Monday, you're moving over to the Navy submarine base where a newly designed boat is waiting and someone to show you what it can do. You will be doing sea trials and only going north, as far as Miami and coming back to the sub base after each run. I'm sure this boat will be an experience and it's the one you'll be taking south. Looking at Jorge and Rafael he said, I'm sorry to have had you come back to Key West for just a few hours, but I'm sure you'll be pleased to hear what I have to say. Take the rest of the week off. In fact why don't the three of you take a mini vacation in Nassau with your wives, all expenses paid".

We looked at John to see if he was kidding, then they looked at me.

"Hey, I said, I know nothing about this.

"It's true", John said. "Don didn't know a thing about this. Though I can't take full credit for this vacation". Then smiling he pointed a finger at me, "Don's company has been doing very well since we put a manager in charge and can easily pay for this vacation. The British Colonial Hotel in Nassau already has reservations for five, as well as Chalks for the flight over and back. I told the Harbor Master to allow you to phone your wives and charge it to me, and the taxi at the pier head has already been paid to take you all back to Chalks in Miami. Have fun, and I'll see you Monday, same time at Chalks. I have to stay here tonight, so have a great weekend,"

With that, he laughed, walked into the galley and poured himself a cup of coffee.

After Jorge and Rafael called their wives, we piled into the taxi, relaxed and enjoyed the five-hour trip back to Chalks, where their wives were already waiting with luggage to board the flight to Nassau.

My accountant must have cringed when our bill came home to roost.

My only regret was that Maria could not have been with us to enjoy Nassau. With the friendly banter and all the girl talk about women's fashion, she would have enjoyed it.

Monday morning we flew back to Key West in a subdued state. Not much was said about the weekend, each absorbed within their own thoughts. John was waiting for us with a car and drove us directly to the sub base. We walked out on a pier and there it was.

A 50-foot boat, noted for speed, endurance, and sea worthiness. We looked at the boat, looked at each other, nodded in agreement, and jumped on board.

Our new boat was a delight, deep "V" hull, long and slender, with all the power of a craft that won many offshore races, not only along the Eastern Seaboard but across the Gulf Stream to the Bahamas. Because of its speed and durability, this boat was also being used by the Federal Drug Enforcement Agency of the government for drug interdiction along the Florida and Gulf Coasts.

John saw the pleased look on our faces, smiled and said, "As I mentioned last week, you're not doing the sea trials south towards Cuba, but north towards Miami. This way anyone watching the boat will think it's working with the DEA on drug enforcement."

When the Gulf Stream moving east, passes Key West and starts going north, it drifts closer to the Florida Coast. The light green warm waters of the Straits of Florida turn to emerald green then take on the dark, deep blue of the Gulf Stream. Most of the time the waves are long, low, stately swells that could easily lull you to sleep. At idling speed the boat would climb up the back of a wave, reach the top and gently slide down its' face only to part the next oncoming wave with its' bow giving a soft, low swishing sound as it passed along the hull to the stern.

At other times, the weather turned nasty and the seas kicked up with the ocean rolling and breaking with white caps and the water, black as the low hanging clouds. With wind driven rain coming down in a tropical deluge, lightning flashes hitting the sea around us and thunder rumbling across the skies, we pushed the boat to its maximum speed to find its limits. Skipping from the white crest of one giant wave to the crest of the next with the shrill scream of the propellers at full throttle lifting out of the water was living on the edge. The word, "exhilarating" could not come close to describe the feeling.

When the hull landed, the sound of it hitting a wave was as if someone hit a base drum, the vibration jarring every bone in your body. Spray would soar fifty feet in the air to be immediately carried away by the wind. These were the times you sat with your seat belt as tight as possible around you, and your kidney belt pulled even tighter. Rain spray would seem to be coming horizontally at you from the speed, hitting your face like hail and you would feel thankful you remembered to bring your safety glasses. You had the feeling you were personally challenging the gods themselves.

On lazy days, we drifted in towards a beach on one of the Florida Keys.

Anchoring in shallow water, we would take turns swimming to the beach, finding a grocery store then swimming back to the boat with a six pack of beer and sandwiches in a watertight bag. We let the boat slowly rock back and forth, making idle, relaxed chatter that happens between three friends or we would just lie back enjoying the day until we headed back to base. In the back of our minds, even though we did not express it, lay a cold blanket that even the Florida sun couldn't pierce—our mission.

After two weeks of sea trials, we headed south to Cuba and our meeting with destiny.

I voluntarily stopped recording and looked at Don. Don looked back at me with a quizzical look on his face.

"What's wrong?" he asked. "Batteries finally run out?"

"No, the batteries are ok, but your story isn't only about people's s lives that touched you but is a part of history. If you don't mind Don, I'd like to take a few minutes to digest some of this."

"Sure, take your time."

I ordered another coffee for both of us and sat back looking through Don's diary. The wind had kicked up again, and with it, a light snow was falling.

"Don, you look exhausted. Why don't I drive you home and we can continue this tomorrow or if a Nor'easter is coming, in a day or so?"

We both were startled as a good-sized branch hit the window.

"You have an excellent plan. I'd appreciate a drive home in this weather and give me a telephone call tomorrow, however I'm doing this with one condition," Don said.

"Sure, just name it."

"You take the diary home with you."

"Don, I don't want the responsibility of doing that."

"Then it's no deal I trust you and I'm trusting you with my most precious possession, my life."

I wanted to get my friend home before a real storm blew in, so after a few minutes agreed to take Don home and keep the diary, as he asked.

Between the rain, sleet, and wind, the drive to Don's house was a challenge. He invited me in to have a cup of tea and to meet his housekeeper. Since he needed assistance with his walker and help to the door, I accepted. His home was decorated simply in early American pine furniture and his housekeeper, Mrs. Neilson, was a cherubic, seventy year old woman that doted on him like a mother. I took to her immediately.

Returning home, I poured myself a glass of Port wine, settled into my favorite reading chair and put on a classical record of Wagner that to me, perfectly fit the mood of the wild night outdoors and the tone of Don's diary.

CHAPTER 19

DON'S STORY (CONT.)

New Jersey, 1961

Time passed and I was still feeling responsible for the deaths of Jorge and Rafael. There was no way to contact anyone in my Cuban family or, for that matter, anyone in Cuba. There was no way for an American to visit Cuba or a Cuban to get to the United States, unless by rubber raft over 90 miles of open sea. Each country was sealed tight against the other. As in any military regime coming into power, Cuba under Castro was no different. Any Cuban denouncing someone for being pro-Batista whether true or not, was considered a hero, with the accused, without a fair trial, severely punished or shot.

With everything I had accomplished business-wise, I felt empty without Maria. There was no joy in success without someone to share it with. Not a day passed that she wasn't in my mind, or at my side. Every time a woman walked by that used her perfume, walked like her, or laughed like her, brought back memories.

The slight Cuban accent when she spoke English, her sense of humor, the spontaneity when she saw something new or unusual. I even missed how she looked when she was angry. I missed the totality of her.

Since I returned to my company, even my feeling about business has changed. I knew part of it was missing Maria, but a bigger part was my two friends at the bottom of the Straits. Business no longer held my interest. Having my own plane, a sport fishing boat or a growing bank account didn't have the same thrill, excitement, or importance or pleasure it once had, they now assumed a place in my life as toys. I was a person totally filled with remorse that had no interest in the future but was harboring all the past guilt feelings of about leaving Cuba, leaving the family, leaving Maria, surviving when my friends died, and taking husbands away from their wives and children.

Winter came and now was slowly leaving. The weather wasn't as severe and some hardy bare branches were sprouting buds. The sky was clear, and like a lemming, I felt the need to get to the ocean, to see the vast expanse of open sea, to smell it, to taste it in the air, and watch the spray as it hit a seawall. So there I was, sitting on a concrete bench on a desolate part of the Jersey shore, as far away as I could possibly be from people, sipping a cup of black coffee. For hours, I watched the sandpipers run in and out of the water's edge and the seaweed and other winter's debris stretched out along the shoreline, slowly being pushed in by the incoming tide. My mind drifting rapidly over a thousand things and yet nothing. I was far, far, away.

Then some sound or movement intruded into my privacy, and realized someone was speaking to me from the other end of the bench. Upset and ready to jump on whoever invaded my daydreams, I turned and there sat John.

"Hi Don, haven't seen you in quite some time," he said. "Sorry about how everything turned out and I'm sure that you've had enough of me for a while. Before I came up this way, I visited Jorge and Rafael's wives to see how they were doing. Rafael's children have grown and are in school. Jorge's wife had a little girl. She named her Isabella after Jorge's mother. The insurance from the Group was enough to cover their expenses until the kids get into college. They are all adjusting to the situation and no, they didn't ask about you."

I looked at him.

"Thanks, you made my day, now who do you want me to kill this time?"

"Come on Don, you know on these operations you never know how it's going to end up and by the way, you look terrible."

"John, stop the small talk and bull! What do you want? How did you find me?"

"I understand you haven't been paying attention to business for over a year.

Perhaps you need a change of business and a change of scenery."

"Are your friends still overseeing my business, and that now includes my health?"

"No," John said, "the end of the operation was the end of our interest in the business. As far as your health, that is a personal observation, since I always look after my friends. To answer your other question, you're too valuable for us to lose so we have a telepathist in Washington monitoring your brain waves keeping us informed of your every thought and location," he said with a smile.

"John, how long ago did you put a tracking device on my car?"

John looked at me, smiled, ignored my question and said, "Don, let me start again. Why not start a small business some-where else where you're completely involved and have no time to think about things that have happened in the past that you cannot control?"

I knew he was right about that, so I said, "So John, where and what kind of business would you suggest?"

"Well, for starters, say southern Florida, Dade, or Broward County, and as for a new business, real estate seems to be in an upward spiral, only the start-up and paper work is very time con-suming. Then again, maybe you enjoy wallowing in your own mis-ery, enjoying that 'poor me' attitude."

This last remark woke me up. "Yeah, and what's the hook in it for you?"

"O.K.," John said" Let me lay it out for you."

"With the closing down of gambling in Havana, pressure is being put on politicos to open casinos along the East Coast, West Coast and around the Mississippi area, but that's not the real problem. The real problem is the two-way traffic of running drugs into the States and dollars back to South and Central American governments.

Castro is behind it with his partner Che Guevara. They want to turn every government in Central and South America red. Already Russia's buddy, China, have more banks in Panama than the Panamanians do and Che Guevara in already starting trouble in several Central and South American countries."

I held up my hand for him to stop talking.

"John we've known each other for a few years. You've never lied to me nor me to you. Truthfully, I don't know what I want and you know something, I don't give a damn about drugs or what happens in Central and South America. All I feel is guilty as hell about what happened and how to make it up to Jorge and Rafael's families. My head is all mixed up, but you are right about the business. I don't care if it stands or falls. I hate even the thought of people being dependent on me, even the people who were with me since I started. I just want to be by myself to come and go as I please, to answer to no one, to be responsible for no one. Do you understand?"

John sat there, just listening, not saying a word, absorbing everything I said. The serenity I was looking for, alone at the ocean was broken, so I rose, as John did, and said, "Let's go have lunch and talk about something else."

From Sandy Hook, the northern tip of the New Jersey shoreline to Cape May at the southern tip is approximately 120 miles. There's a paved road running parallel to the beach most of the way, and on the side away from the ocean, there is at least one bar-restaurant for every four stores. The exception is winter when there's perhaps one store open every two miles and a bar-restaurant every twenty. Where we were sitting was one of those twenty-mile stretches of quiet desolation.

"John, get in my car and I'll take you to one of my favorite seafood houses that's open, if that's ok with you?"

"Sure", he said. "You buying or crying?"

"Hell John, since you can't afford it, I'll buy."

We had lunch at 'Angelo's Fish Net', a seafood house I knew that was known for its excellent food, good drinks, fair prices, and open all year round. After a satisfying lunch and a few drinks, that were made more enjoyable by the wind against the rattling windows, watching white caps on the ocean, and close to a roaring fireplace, all my senses were dulled. John, looked at me, smiled and placed a business card in my hand, saying, "Don, with that telephone number you can reach me anytime, so when you feel ready, don't hesitate to use it."

John left; I had another scotch and sat at one of the outside tables. It was cold and windy, but that was perfect since I had the patio to myself and could still see the ocean. On the horizon the white sails of a sailboat were moving parallel to the coast and in my head it portrayed my life over the last few years, visible yet untouchable. I looked down at the business card John gave me before he left; it had only his name and a telephone number on it, no address or title.

My conversation with John played repeatedly in my mind. After another scotch, I decided to put it all aside until I could think more clearly, believing in the old axiom, "When in doubt-don't." I asked for the check, gave the waiter my credit card, added a tip, signed it, got up and walked to my car. It was already twilight and the temperature was dropping. Spring was still a long way off. John was right! I was wallowing in my misery and not facing reality.

Several weeks passed, I knew that John was giving me time to think the subject through without any pressure from him. Any decision was totally my own, with no input from anyone. One evening, after having with dinner with friends, I returned to my office to tie up some loose odds and ends. All the employees had gone home several hours before and there I sat with a yellow legal pad in front of me, to list the pros and cons of where I was and where I could be. After an hour all I had covering the paper was a mass of doodles. One phone call to John could change all that, but that one phone call could also change into another fiasco with people getting hurt or dying.

"John was right," I said aloud to no one. "I need to get out of this rut, and a complete change will do me good." I lifted the phone, dialed the number, and was immediately put through to John.

"John, sorry to bother you at this time of night. Where are you located geographically?"

"That's a stupid question," replied John. "I'm in bed."

"No, no," I replied. "Are you in Washington?"

"I'm in Miami," he said. "And what's the urgency of the call?"

"John, "you were right; I need a complete change. Book me a room at the hotel where you are staying and I'll call you when I get in this afternoon."

That afternoon at five, I was sitting in John's hotel room overlooking Biscayne Bay.

John poured two scotches, turned and said, "Out of curiosity, what brought you to your decision?"

I looked at him and replied, "You were right. I need a complete change but before I do anything or make any moves, I need something from you. Then and only then am I willing to listen to your plan."

"And what is it you need from me, Don?"

"I need closure. I need to see Maria and my son and see if there is a possibility of getting them into the States. Also, I need to find out what happened to her mother and father, maybe even find a way to get them all out of Cuba as well."

"You're crazy. You know the only way to do that is by boat, and with everything that's happened, plus the Russians, it would be impossible."

"No John, I think I have a plan."

John, standing by the picture window, turned around and said, "O.K. let's hear the impossible."

"Canada and Cuba have no problems. Canadians fly back and forth to Cuba every week. If you get me a passport in an assumed name, as an independent member of the Canadian Health Commission, I could get in. I would use the premise that I wanted to compare pediatric Canadian health care to theirs. Maria is one of the leading pediatricians, and with your influence you could arrange my meeting with her at her hospital under this assumed name."

John thought it through, smiled and said, "Let me see what I can do. I'm not promising anything, but if this works out, you will owe me big time."

"John old buddy, if it works out, you'll be the best man at my wedding."

We went to my favorite restaurant on Calle Ocho for dinner. I stayed the night at the hotel he booked, and left the next morning to put the company up for sale.

The adage, "What goes around comes around," was true. Within a month I had an offer from someone I casually knew and who had once helped when I was in the olive oil business. He had also moved into general contracting when the olive oil business came under investigation. I accepted the offer and made my decision to move on. I kept John apprised of the sale of the business and told him that with all the personal things I had to get in order for me to move to Miami, I was going to keep my apartment in New Jersey until I returned from Cuba. Selling the business was the first part, the second, moving out of the area. Most of all I wanted the future to have no ties with anyone or anything from the past. I wanted to start fresh.

A few weeks later, while going over details with the new owners, a secretary came in and said there was a gentleman at the reception desk who wanted to see me. I excused myself and walked to the reception area, where a trim young man with a military haircut, dressed in civilian clothes was waiting. As I entered, he stood and asked, "Are you Don?"

"Yes."

"May I please see some identification?"

"Sure, let me get it for you."

The young man scrutinized the documents, seemed satisfied, then handed over the small package, saluted and left. I immediately knew whom it was from. I put the sealed package in my briefcase anxiously waiting to leave for the day so I could open it when I was home alone. It would be interesting to see what John Smith had accomplished. It was all there, a Canadian passport, a Cuban visa and documentation with my new Canadian name and address, as well as, business cards and business documents. Also, enclosed were Delta Airline tickets from Newark Airport to Toronto, Canada, Canadian Air from Toronto to Havana, and return. The final leg being United airlines from Toronto back to Newark. Included was a hospital schedule with names and times of duty for medical doctors with their specialties, Canadian money, and a reservation at the Hotel Nacional. Underneath everything was a handwritten note,

Don, To meet your schedule, the tickets are undated. You need to make the final arrangements. The day you leave Canada call me so I can follow up with the rest of the plan. Stay at the Nacional for one day to rest. On the second day I will arrange for an appointment at 10 am with Maria. Call this hospital number to confirm.

After that, you are on your own.

Good luck. JS

John's part of the bargain was complete. Now it was up to me to coordinate dates and times. To prevent anyone connecting an American with the flight to Cuba, I dialed Canadian air in Newark and was told they only make the trip to Cuba twice a week from Toronto. They gave me the day but I did not want to make the reservation until I could make the call from Toronto. To get me there, I called Delta and made a reservation to arrive in Toronto a day before. I was playing it as safe as possible, two different passports, and two different names.

I looked at the clock. It was going on six in the morning but I could not put Don's diary down. It was hard to believe my elderly, placid friend could have been involved with the Government, the CIA, or a Cuban group in Miami trying to overthrow Castro.

I wondered about Maria and Don's son. Where are they now? Is she still involved in medicine or is she retired, or even alive? What happened to her Mama, Papa, and Aunt Clara? The boy must be a teenage and be interesting to see if he resembles Don? Did Maria ever tell him his father was American? A thousand, no a million questions, and scenarios formed in my mind.

I got up to stretch and walked over to the window. By this time, dawn would be breaking, but as I pulled the curtain aside, snow was falling and the roads and sidewalks were already covered in white. Our Nor-Easter had arrived.

Passing my bedroom, the bed looked inviting but the diary was like a magnet, pulling me back into the story.

CHAPTER 20

HAVANA

A week later, I landed in Toronto and called John. My plane was leaving in two hours. For the first time I used my new name and passport going through Canadian Customs. Waiting two hours in the Terminal to board my flight to Havana was nerve wracking and I'm sure the amount of coffee I consumed didn't help. When I finally heard the boarding call, any adventure I had experienced in the past paled in comparison to what I was about to attempt.

The flight from Toronto to Havana was both boring, due to the number of hours in the air, but exciting with the thought of seeing Maria again after three years. Thinking of her vastly over-shadowed the fears of what might happen to me going through Cuban Customs now that the Russian military had a presence in Cuba.

Has she changed? Are our feelings towards each other going to be same? Can I somehow get them all out of Cuba? Does she even want to leave? My emotions were in turmoil as minute by minute the plane drew closer to Havana.

Then, over the loud speaker, "Passengers, please fasten your seat belts we are preparing to land". Ladies and gentlemen, we ask your cooperation. The Cuban government requires all planes landing in Havana to have their window shades closed. Thank you."

One didn't have to be skilled in military operations to figure out the logic behind this request from the flight attendant. The reasoning behind this is when coming in for a landing, the passengers would not only be able to see and count the Russian types of aircraft parked all over the airport, but where dug in anti-aircraft guns were placed.

The plane landed and all the happy, joking vacationers lined up to get off. We then walked through a cordon of military police on the tarmac, lining up once more in the terminal to go through customs. I was surprised to see the number of Russian soldiers with submachine guns scattered throughout the transition area, as well as the tight discipline imposed upon the new arrivals. What bothered me was the way officials at Customs were interrogating each Canadian. It sounded more like an inquisition than them being pleased that tourists were bringing hard cash into Cuba.

Unexpectedly, a guard came over and placed his hand on my arm. My heart stopped for a moment, "Senor, you are not with the tour group, you have to come with me."

His tone of voice wasn't one of request, but one of command. With his hand still on my arm, he escorted me over to a Cuban customs agent sitting with a Russian official.

These weren't the friendly, happy go lucky Cubans I knew or was used to. These were serious, suspicious, hard-eyed men who at one time either were police officers or trained by the Russians in interrogation.

Behind each agent's station was a two way glass mirror demonstrating the seriousness of their customs process. Without doubt, Cubans and Russians were double checking both the arrivals and their own custom agents, observing and listening to everything.

My turn came up. No welcome to Cuba! No good afternoon! No pleasantries!

Just, "why are you here?" spoken in broken English.

I laid my passport, visa, and documents on the desk.

"As you can see I'm an independent contractor for the Canadian Government. My documents show that I am doing research on Health Care programs in various countries to help improve our Canadian system."

"Have you ever been in Cuba before?"

"No Sir."

"Have you any friends in Cuba?"

"No Sir."

"I see by your passport, you never travelled or did this study in any other country before Cuba" the Russian agent stated, slowly turning the passport pages.

"Cuba is the closest country to Canada with this type of health care system."

"Why did you pick the Hotel Nacional?"

"I didn't, my government did."

"Another question senor," he asked, "do you speak Spanish?"

"No Sir," I replied.

Since I boarded the plane in Toronto I spoke only English, and to fellow passengers I limited it to, "yes, no, please and thank you". I found it was always better to know a foreign language and feign ignorance so you know what people around you are saying, than to open your mouth and get involved in a story that may trip you later, more so, when you do not know who you are talking to.

The Russian customs agent turned to the Cuban and in Spanish asked him if he wanted to ask me any further questions. The Cuban looked at me and was just about to open his mouth, when there was a knock on the one-way mirror. He rose from his chair, said "no," and walked away. By this time my mouth was so dry it was an effort to talk, and between the temperature in the terminal and my nerves, I was sweating like the proverbial pig.

"Bien, senor," the Agent said as he stamped and returned my passport, Visa, and documents. I mentally breathed a deep sigh of relief. The first step was over. I was back in Cuba and much closer to Maria, but I could feel eyes on my back as I followed the tourists out the terminal door where they went into the waiting hotel bus while I decided to take a taxi. The rational by being alone, there was no need to make conversation with anyone.

The ride to the hotel was uneventful. I gave the driver my destination in English and settled back in the seat to see the changes in Havana since I had left. The streets were littered with garbage and potholes everywhere. All the buildings I passed that were made of wood and in need of repair and painting. Most importantly, since the new regime being backed by Russia, the lines at food stores seemed endless, with people waiting in long lines to get in. The taxi driver was constantly looking in the rearview mirror speaking in English interspersed with Spanish. I answered his broken English remarks with one word responses or a shrug of my shoulders and I'm sure his job is such that he is required reports back to someone anything he hears odd or suspicious from any passenger in his taxi.

Driving up the small hill to the entrance of the Hotel Nacional started to bring back pleasant memories of earlier times. It was built in the 1930's, with art deco features mixed with the Spanish-Morrish architecture had not changed, but it was sorely in need of painting and masonry work. I was surprised, that while the buildings needed restoration, the gardens were as beautiful as I remembered, with the two cannons still sitting in its center.

Hard to believe that in October of 1933 Batista was involved with other junior officers in a revolt against the privileges of high ranking officers that listened only to the interests of another ousted president, Gerardo Machado, and now Batista is gone and his place has been taken over by Castro.

When I registered at the hotel, I was told that the Defense Committee of the Revolution and visiting dignitaries occupied the majority of the hotel. Revolution or not, I thought, hard currencies from outside Cuba are still needed whether in rubles, dollars, francs or pounds and with cash, rooms are always available.

The bellhop was given the key to my room from the reception desk, he lifted my valise, and we took one of the ancient, creaking elevators to my sixth floor ocean front room. As he opened the door to my room, I stepped in and my attention was immediately drawn to the windows. It was breathtaking! I could see Morro Castle guarding the entrance to Havana harbor and beyond that the sea. Walking closer to the windows and looking down was the sea wall where small children were still running to and away from the ocean spray breaking over the rocks. I smiled to myself, their time of innocents, too young to know what life was about. All this time, the bellhop was keeping up a one sided dialog in Spanish interspersed with phrases in English which I completely ignored. It only stopped when I turned and tipped him. Now alone I looked around the room. The room was in need of repair, wallpaper was hanging in spots around the windows due to rain seepage. The ceilings were at least 10 feet high. Crown and floor moldings that could not be duplicated, were water stained. Massive furniture of some dark wood that must be as old as the hotel were chipped, cracked and in some cases splintered. In the bathroom, the faucet handles were rusted and the tap water ran only cold. Taking a shower would be a challenge in a bathtub that you could swim in and was elevated from the floor by big cast iron paws held up from the floor. I was happy to find a bar of soap in my luggage from the Canadian hotel I stayed at before I flew here and my one regret was that I should have also taken one of their towels. The towels I was looking at were hanging on a rusted rack looked thin, raggedy and not to clean looking.

I hung my clothes up in the closet, hoping that my clothes wouldn't absorb the musty smell of dampness and dust from years of only superficial house cleaning. I lay down on the bed, comfortable with clean sheets but my last thoughts were it had the same musty odor as the rest of the room.

I did nothing but sleep on and off the first day in Havana. I never left the room and called room service for my meals. The anticipation of seeing Maria tomorrow slowed the clock on my night table to where every minute seemed like an hour. Finally the morning came. My phone rang; it was my six o'clock wakeup call. This was the day I had waited years for. I shaved, showered, dressed carefully, and felt that if I went down for breakfast, being with other people would help me lose some of this feeling of anticipation and nervousness.

The dining room was the same as I remembered. Only now, it looked aged and uncared for, as did the lobby and the rest of the hotel. I ordered scrambled eggs, toast, and coffee and looking around, noted the preponderance of Cuban and Russian military uniforms in the room. When the food arrived, too nervous to eat, I pushed the food around on the plate and returned to my room. For the tenth time since six A.M., I checked the directions to the hospital, looked myself over in the mirror, opened the hotel room door, and went on the quest that would determine the rest of my life.

To relieve the tension in my mind, I walked the few blocks to the hospital not appreciating the warmth of the sun or the singing of the birds and oblivious to everything other than what I was going to say to Maria. I never even bothered to check if anyone was following me. Surely, a super-spy I was not.

Ten minutes before the interview time my supposed Canadian Government Agency had set up for me with the Head Administrator, I was standing in front of the hospital. The thought popped into my head that this must be the same dread feeling a prisoner must have walking the last mile before he's executed.

The hospital covered an entire city block. It was made of stone in the bygone era when buildings were made to last and their entrances as ornate as an architect could design them. From years of exposure to the damp sea air and the tropical sun, the stone had a fine patina of moss covering parts of the walls. The concrete walks were interspersed with fountains, and all led to the marble steps leading up to its grand entrance.

At the top of the stairs an armed guard opened the wrought iron gate for me and, not speaking English, pointed to the receptionist desk that was located in the center of the lobby. The leather heels of my shoes made a distinctive clicking sound as I walked over the tiled floor causing a few heads to turn my way, thereby, adding to my self-consciousness. I handed her my business card.

"Would you please tell Dr. Barca that Mr. Belmont from Canada is here for his appointment."

Apparently, she understood English. The young lady took my card, checked her appointment book and lifted her phone to speak to someone. Nodding her head a few times she replaced the phone in its cradle, rose from her desk, and asked me to follow her.

Knocking on a large wooden door at the other side of the hall, she opened it, announced my name and then allowed me to enter.

Standing behind his desk was a short heavyset man with a big smile on his face. He came around the desk with his hand out ready for me to shake, and said in perfect English;

"Senor Belmont, I'm Dr. Barca. On behalf of Cuba and myself, I'm very pleased to meet you. Please have a seat. May I offer you coffee or a glass of cold water perhaps?"

We shook hands and for a moment the warmth and graciousness of old Cuba nearly made me reply in Spanish. Fortunately, my brain kicked in and stopped my tongue. We chatted about health care in both countries for a few minutes and then he said, "Unfortunately I have an appointment I cannot cancel and have to leave. I hope your short stay in our Country will be pleasant, informative and educational.

However, since you don't speak Spanish and my knowledge of English is unfortunately poor, I have just the right person to take you around and explain what we do. She spent much time in the States and speaks English perfectly. The patients call her their angel. Our Maria is tireless and her knowledge is phenomenal. Here is one person completely dedicated to helping children. Angelina, please escort Senor Belmont to Dr. Rodriguez's office. It's right down the hallway. I would take you there myself, but as I said, I have an important meeting, so please forgive me."

We both got up, shook hands and I exited Dr. Barca's office with Angelina.

A feeling of love, anticipation, fear, happiness and every emotion a human could ever feel or have, swept over me. The culmination of years of planning and our future as a family was only a few minutes and steps away.

CHAPTER 21

The receptionist walked me down the hall, pointed to a door, knocked, opened it and announced, "Mr. Belmont from Canada is here for his 10 o'clock appointment."

I thanked her, walked in and made sure to close the door behind me.

Sitting behind her desk, with the sunlight shining on her from a side window, was Maria, looking more mature, more composed, more beautiful than when I first met her.

She looked more like a model than a doctor. I had complete meltdown. All the love I had came back in one great rush.

Maria stared at me and rubbed her eyes several time. Looked at me again, took a step, stumbled, put one hand over her mouth, and reached out with the other for her desk to steady herself. Inadvertently, her hand hit a picture frame that smashed on the floor. I glanced down and amid the broken glass was a picture of a three or four year old boy with blond hair and blue eyes. Isn't it strange, I can still close my eyes and see the picture landing and breaking on a yellow and soft blue ceramic tile floor. I glanced at it for a second then raised my eyes to Maria.

"Si Querida, it's me."

I opened my arms to embrace her, to bury my face in her hair, to taste her lips against mine and her body against me, to turn back the years.

Suddenly her look of astonishment and disbelief turned to recognition then to one of unsuppressed anger. The vein on her temple popped out as it always did when she was angry. Maria put her fingers to her lips and pointed to the walls. I understood immediately. I walked to her, my arms outstretched to hold her in my arms. When I was close she held out one arm and stopped me with her hand on my chest. I knew she could feel my heart beating. Shaking her head, she looked at me and said one word, "No!"

She backed away, lifted her right hand, pointed, and said, "Murderer, how dare you come here after killing my brother and then my mother.

We welcomed you into our family, into our home, I welcomed you into my arms and death is the thanks you gave in return."

The greeting was something I never, never expected. I was speechless . My mind could not function. Did she recognize me? I did not know what to say.

"Maria, it's me. It's Don."

"I know very well who you are and more important what you are—a murderer.

I blame you for killing Jorge and Mamazita.

I want nothing to do with you. Leave here immediately or I'm calling the guard and I'll see you shot."

"Maria, please, please wait," I pleaded, "I risked my life to come here, to take you and our son back to the States."

"No waiting- Leave this minute! Understand! I want nothing to do with you, and I will be happy to hear when you are as dead as my family. Go immediately!

I'm serious about calling the guard."

Every time I raised my hand to stop her from speaking, she slapped it down. It was useless trying to speak or reason with her.

I pointed to the picture on the floor surrounded by shattered glass.

"Is that our son?"

"That is my son."

She walked back to her desk, put her hand on the telephone phone and said, "This is your last chance. Go or get shot. That is your choice."

I turned, feeling completely empty, opened her office door, and walked out. She slammed the door behind me. Closing the door to her office, closed all the dreams I had for planning our future together. I vaguely remember passing the receptionist and walking out of the hospital. It wasn't only rejection building up in me, but anger that I risked my life to come all this way and not be given the opportunity to explain what had happened or to try to take her and our family to a better, freer life. My reward was a slap in my face and a stab to my heart.

The entire trip, all my plans, all my dreams, went up in smoke. I was weighted down with hurt, rejection, anger and complete emptiness as I walked back to the Nacional, never realizing a storm had come in and how heavy it was raining or how wet I was. My life had just turned from expectations of what could be, to one again without meaning. My dreams and hopes now ashes.

I was scheduled to fly out in two days, so I had a lot of empty time to rethink everything that just happened, to go over every word spoken at least a dozen times. The constant thought that intruded was that of the child that Jorge said I fathered, the little boy in the broken picture frame. The child's coloration was the same as mine as were the blue eyes and blond hair. In my heart, I knew he was my son. I again pictured her standing there alongside her desk, angrily pointing her right hand, yelling at me and telling me to go. It was then I realized that my ID bracelet still encircled her wrist. I was now positive it was our son, but angry and perplexed as to why she didn't hear me out and forced me to leave.

Back in the hotel room I thought more about the time we had been apart, all the things that we had not shared. Did she ever think about or miss me? Was the boy healthy?

Was he in school? So many questions flew through my mind; questions upon questions that I realized would always remain unanswered. Then my thoughts drifted in another direction.

How easy it would be for Maria, filled with anger as she was, to call the authorities saying I had come into Cuba as a Canadian citizen, with a false name, a forged Canadian Passport and under false pretense. It would be simple for them to find the hotel where I was staying. In fact, the receptionist at the hospital mentioned the Nacional while we were speaking. I desperately hoped, after her anger passed, she would reconsider everything and come to me at the hotel, alone or with our son.

Exhausted, angry and upset, I sat looking out of my hotel window, which was too high to see a person's individual features, yet hoping to see Maria's distinctive walk or a woman holding a child's hand coming up the stone path leading to the entrance of the Nacional. For two days, I stayed in that room looking out the window. For two days waiting for a knock on the door that would end my Cuban visit one way or another; Maria coming to see me or being thrown into a Cuban jail. Finally, with my time in Cuba running out, I slowly packed my few belongings, zippered my luggage, checked the hotel room one last time and closed the door.

The lobby was full of uniforms, both Cuban and Russian with a sprinkling of uniforms I didn't recognize. I was oblivious and disinterested in what was going on around me when suddenly felt a hand on my arm. Instantly, I was brought back to reality.

I turned and there was a police officer.

"Senor, if you are checking out you must collect your passport and visa at the desk of the Policia here at the hotel."

Fortunately, I had the intelligence and presence of mind to respond in English saying that I didn't understand him. He repeated his statement in English, walked me to the reception desk and offered to call me a taxi to take me to the airport. I mentally shook myself. The situation I was in was only for a few more hours. I had best keep my wits about me and put everything else aside until the plane was in the air and outside of Cuban jurisdiction.

The taxi took me to the airport where again the hope arose that Maria and maybe Maria and the baby would be waiting for me in the terminal. I checked my luggage and must have walked the terminal at least four times, covering every store, every aisle, every seat. No Maria. Finally, my flight was called. I walked through my last barrier, Customs, ignoring the one-way mirrors in the walls. My visa and passport were handed back to me without incident and when the Russian soldier, practicing his English, asked me how I enjoyed my stay in Cuba, my response was the same as every tourist, "Yes, my trip to Cuba was very enjoyable."

We lined up for the plane in the terminal, walked across the tarmac single file as we did when we arrived, and again through a squad of soldiers on both sides of us. Then we climbed the rolling stairs into the aircraft. I have no idea how anyone else felt, but just boarding that Air Canada plane released a big knot in my stomach, knowing that hopefully in a few minutes we would be airborne without incident but my plan, my life had ended .

I sat in my assigned seat alongside a window. The shades were lowered as they were required to be on landing, deep in my own thoughts, completely disregarding the person who sat down beside me. I was definitely in no mood to make conversation with anyone in English, Spanish or any other language. Then as they were closing the aircraft's door, one last thought popped into my head. Will she ever tell our son about me?

The engines came to life, we lined up with the runway, and with a surge of power I started my 1,500-mile flight to Toronto, 1,000 miles back to New Jersey, and then another 1,000 miles to Miami. A total of 3,500 miles. How ironic, since there's only 150 miles from where I'm sitting on this Havana runway, to Miami, my final destination.

The flight to Toronto was uneventful, I dozed most of the way. In Toronto, I went to Barclay's Bank where I had rented a safe deposit box before I left and retrieved my American passport and driver's license. Since my plane wasn't leaving for New Jersey until the next morning, I spent the night in a hotel, where I tore up and burned my Canadian passport and Cuban Visa in an ashtray. Then to make sure there was no evidence of anyone with that name having gone to Cuba, I flushed them both down the commode.

My flight to Newark left on time and the pain of what happened with Maria in Cuba was lessening. I had to get on with my life and was looking forward to winding things up and starting a new life in Florida. From what I'd been reading, John was right about going into real estate. The economy of Florida had been growing rapidly with the arrival of Cubans that had brought money.

Money was also coming in from other South American countries because their nationals felt that their countries, politically, may be going the way of Cuba and needed a safe haven. In addition, a few astute American investors realized what was happening and wanted a piece of the future. My friend Mario was right.

CHAPTER 22

Newark was smog bound from the number of industrial factories it had, and there was a slight drizzle falling. I found my car in the airport parking lot, paid for the few days it was there, and took route 95 heading south to my home in Rumson.

A few miles south, I saw the tractor-trailer skidding across the lane towards my car, and vaguely remember turning the wheel. I knew nothing after that until I woke up in the hospital.

Sometime later, it may have been a week or more, I heard someone calling my name. I opened my eyes reluctantly and there, standing alongside my bed was John.

"Hey old buddy, glad to see you're still with us."

"John, what happened? I hurt all over. How long have I been in here?"

"Well to answer your questions, your car was completely demolished by a tractor trailer. You are going to be hospitalized for several more weeks. You have been broken up considerably and you have been unconscious for a week. We didn't think you would make it."

"How did you know I was here?"

"You're our star. We were tracking you since Toronto, making sure you were ok, nevertheless, I guess we did not do such a good job. Anyway, get some rest and I will visit again in a few days."

"How bad am I?"

"Old buddy, I'm no doctor, you'll have to ask him."

With that, he turned and left.

The result of the accident was a spinal fracture that was treated with surgery and physical therapy. The result was that there would be a residual limp with limited mobility and use of my arms and hands. Getting around would require assistance of a walker or scooter and pain would be my constant companion for the rest of my life.

After being discharged, I returned home and hired a full time housekeeper. I spent every waking hour looking for a place in the United States where I wanted to spend the rest of my life, as far away from New Jersey and Florida as possible. Principally, the criteria was to be near the ocean and in small village. Then one day, looking through a brochure on Maine, I came across the village of East Harbor. John took the trip with me. He drove, while I stretched out in the back of the car to alleviate some of the pain. The village was everything I was looking for.

Driving back to New Jersey, John told me that his group would take care of any financial expenses I incurred. He then used the same phase Mario Ruggiero had said a long time ago, "You only thought you saw and heard what you did."

After he drove me back to New Jersey, we never spoke or saw each other again.

CHAPTER 23

1970

❧

MAINE

I completed the last page of Don's diary and reluctantly, slowly, turned the last page and closed the cover on his life. His heartfelt story was as beautiful as any I had ever read. It must have been horrible to carry a story like his bottled inside him for that many years. The pain of having someone you love and had a child with, turning you away after risking your life, was incomprehensible. I felt Don's pain as if it were my own.

The predicted Nor-easter had arrived. The wind had already started to build snowdrifts alongside houses and branches were being ripped off trees. After I made breakfast I tried to reach Don by phone but according to the radio several communities telephone lines were down, apparently his was one with problems I reread his diary that day and tried reaching him more than once, but his service was still out. I left word that if the snow stopped and the roads were cleared, I was flying out that afternoon to attend a previous appointment and would call him when I returned.

By noon, the storm abated and the road to the airport was reported open. Don had not returned my call and I drove to the airport. I tried to reach him the next day and at least once a day for the entire week I was away. His telephone line was reactivated and when he didn't answer, I left word on his answering machine that I called, explained how many times I tried to reach him and what I thought of his diary.

When I returned, and feeling more than ever that something was wrong, I immediately placed a call Don. Again, the only response was his answering machine so I decided to drive to his home. Pulling into his driveway, I was taken aback! I hadn't seen a black wreath on an entrance door in years.

With mixed feelings, I knocked on the door. It opened, and there, with tears running down her checks was Don's housekeeper, Mrs. Neilson.

"Is Don at home Mrs. Neilson? I've been trying to reach him for days."

"Please come in. I'm so happy to see you. Don is no longer with us. He passed away a week ago from a severe heart attack. I'm cleaning out his affects before his family puts the house up for sale. I tried to telephone you several times after our phone was put back in service after the storm, but you did not answer. Please come in and have a cup of tea with me. The house is so empty. He was like a son and I miss him.

The news hit me hard. Don and I were getting to be very close friends.

"Where is his family holding services?"

"There were no services. They had him cremated the day after he passed on and the same day they already scattered his ashes on the ocean, I am afraid you are too late.

There is something though. He told me that if anything ever happened to him, there was an envelope he wanted me to give you, it is in his desk. Finish your tea while I get it."

Mrs. Neilson came back into the kitchen with Don's briefcase. When I opened it, I found a plain brown envelope and on it was written,

Dear friend, You now have the diary and all my notes, the basis of my story. If you are interested in writing a book, I'm enclosing funds which will enable you to pursue it anyway or anywhere you think it should go.——Or not at all if you so desire.

Bless you. Don

After making small talk with Mrs. Neilson, I rose, kissed her on the cheek, thanked her for the package Don left for me and headed to the *nearest bar. The empty feeling didn't change after several drinks. It was something more than grief or the loss of a friend. I was subconsciously seeking to put closure, to complete Don's story. To close the circle by finding Maria. Don's diary was her legacy not mine. It had to end where it started, in Cuba.*

CHAPTER 24

*T*he more I thought of it, the more excited I became. From an idea, it changed into a compulsion. I had no family. The consultant project I was on was completed. The money was on hand. Like Don, I needed something more than the mundane existence I was living.

Love for a friend? Compulsion? Personal fulfillment? Whatever the reason, whatever the cost, I had to complete his story. A story and life that I now felt I was a part of and obligated to finish. First, if I was going to Cuba to give Maria Don's diary, I needed a copy for myself. More important I needed a game plan to get into Cuba having no thoughts or contacts as to how to go about doing it. .

East Harbor, Maine fortunately was very close to the Canadian Border, and a few days later while doing research in the local library on Cuba, I happened to find a Canadian newspaper. Whether by fate or coincidence, while browsing through the travel section came across a small ad from a snorkeling club on the Cayman Islands, taking qualified divers to Cuba on a one-week excursion and a telephone number to call for more information. An idea immediately formed. Rather than call, why not fly down and get the information on site. My American passport would get me into the Caymans with no problem and I could work things out from there. A few days later, I was in Georgetown, Grand Cayman.

Georgetown was no different from any other large, tourist city in the world. Money may not be able to buy poverty but it certainly has a place in certain sections of the business world. Within a week, I rented a safety box in the Barclay bank where I sequestered my American passport, keys and all other identification until I was returning to the States. In the same week, I found the right people to counterfeit a British passport and a Cuban visa.

The Cayman Islands are noted all over the world for its spectacular underwater coral reefs, so it wasn't difficult to join this International scuba group that held a blanket permit to scuba dive in Cuban water. Two days after I arrived, I was qualified and accepted to join one of their groups. With a British passport, Cuban Visa and hard currency, getting into Cuba was assured.

Our group landed in Havana and I knew before I left the States that I would be confronted with several problems. I didn't speak Spanish as Don did. I never visited Cuba before. Our group would be closely watched and I didn't know what hospital Maria would be working in, or for that matter, if she were still actively working.

The first day we were to dive, I informed the dive master that I was having trouble with my ears and needed to see a doctor. He in turn translated it to our Cuban guide who authorized me to go to the nearest hospital for an examination. Since I didn't know where the hospital was, the Cuban guide escorted me there for an agreed amount of British Pounds, and for a small additional sum, to the head of the line waiting to see a doctor. I was surprised. It seemed the norm for a foreigner with money to be privileged.

After depositing me in the waiting room, my escort inquired if I knew my way back to the hotel and when I said yes, he took off to rejoin the dive group. A doctor, who spoke some English, shrugged his shoulders and said he could not find anything wrong examined me. I thanked him and being on my own, walked back into the waiting room.

Fortunately, one of the nurses spoke some English and was very happy to practice her little knowledge of the language on me. With this friendly rapport, I took a blank sheet of paper and drew a building, printing "hospital" on it. Then I superimposed a pyramid coming out of its sides and at the top printed "Doctor Maria Rodriguez," with a question mark. My newfound friend understood immediately and nodded. She pointed to the door with one hand and moving her fingers in a walking manner with the other. Don must have been looking down from heaven and had something to do with this stroke of luck. Of all the clinics and hospitals in Havana, Maria was located in the Administrative offices on the ground floor of the one I was in.

I walked out of the waiting room into the corridor in the direction the nurse pointed out to me. Being a foreigner and not speaking Spanish, if I were stopped I could say I saw a doctor and was lost. That solved that problem. Out of the corner of my eye, I spotted the receptionist desk off to one side as I walked out the main entrance and back to my hotel. My problem was to formulate some plan to meet Maria. That night at dinner, I told the dive master that the doctor insisted that I could not dive for the remainder of the trip and wanted to see me the next morning. We agreed that I would not request reimbursement for the trip and I'd personally pay all medical or drug expenses I incurred, not the dive company. I was now free to do what I needed to do.

The next morning, at 7:30 a.m., I was sitting in the corridor on a bench a few feet from the receptionist desk. Behind her desk were a few offices with names of the occupants and titles on copper plates affixed to the doors. Dr. Maria Rodriguez office was the second from the right. The door was ajar, she hadn't arrived yet. I had the diary in a plain paper bag on my lap. Anyone noticing me would think it was medicine or my breakfast. I had no idea what she looked like and my game plan was, if someone walked past the receptionist desk into her office, the likelihood was it would be Maria. Again, being a foreigner and not knowing the language would be my "out" if anyone questioned me and I could use the excuse that I needed to see the ear doctor again.

Somewhere in the distance, a church bell started to ring the hour and exactly at eight o'clock, a very attractive woman entered the corridor walking towards me. She looked around Don's age, wearing slacks, and a blouse under an unbuttoned white doctor's jacket. Her hair was black with touches of grey and walked in a way that could only can be described as Don described her as a regal bearing. Instinctively I knew it was Don's Maria.

In English I asked," Dr. Maria Rodriguez?"

She looked at me, startled, and replied in English, "yes."

"Many years ago did you know an American Navy pilot named Don?"

189

She lost all color in her face. Held one arm out to support herself on the corridor wall, the other hand covered her mouth as if to hold back a scream.

I hastily glanced at both her wrists. There was no wedding band on her finger; however, on her right arm an I.D. bracelet encircled her wrist. I opened the paper bag and withdrew the diary.

"I came a long way to give you this. Don passed away a few weeks ago. It is yours to do with as you wish. Don and I were close friends and he wanted me to write a book based on his diary. I'm no writer and I'm sure he would rather you have it."

Maria just stood there and said nothing. She just kept looking at the diary and then back at me. I realized people would start coming in, and it may cause her a problem, so I said, "Take it. I'm staying at the" El Nacional." On a slip of paper, I had already written my name, the hotel's telephone number, my room number and handed it to her.

"I'd love to see you again before I leave. If there is anything more you wish to know, please call and we'll meet somewhere. I leave Cuba in 2 days".

She still did not respond. I took her hand and placed the diary in it. With that, I turned and left. At the end of the corridor, I looked back. Maria was still standing there just as I left her, with Don's diary clutched to her chest staring at me as I walked to the street.

CHAPTER 25

*T*he next morning after breakfast, I returned to my room to plan my day when there was a knock on the door. I opened it and there stood a slender, ramrod straight, elderly man. He whispered in English, could he come in. I opened the door wider, he entered, put out his hand to shake mine and put his other on my shoulder.

"I know who you are, I'm Maria's father," he said. "The walls in Cuba have ears so I can only say this once. When you leave the hotel, make a left and two streets from here is a restaurant named Eduardos. You needn't be too concerned about being followed since, for a few blocks in this "tourist zone", the Cuban Government wants you to think the country is still a democracy and tourist are free to move about. Wear your wristwatch on your right wrist with the watch face upside down, so you can be identified. Go to the rear of the restaurant and someone will be there to take you to Maria. Be there promptly at 5."

With that, he shook my hand again and left. The remainder of the day dragged along. Fortunately, I had Spanish language tapes to listen to, to pass the time until my appointment.

At the hotel's front desk, I collected my passport and Visa and, as I read in all spy stories, slowly walked down the street looking into every store window and then behind me to see if I was being followed. It was my third day in Havana and it first dawned on me the number of armed soldiers patrolling the streets, even in this tourist section of Havana. The stores were loaded with merchandise from Russia, China and some African countries as shown by the masks, spears and other trinkets all displayed for the tourist. Local citizens were not allowed to purchase any of this merchandise and the only currencies accepted by these stores were foreign currencies. Every telephone street pole had a picture of Castro, Raul or Guevara nailed to it. Cuban flags were hanging from every window. Revolutionary slogans were painted on many buildings. Streets were without litter but potholes were many and what cars were moving were ancient, with well-worn tires. Benches were freshly painted. What lawns there were, were trimmed. The sound of soft Latin music came from every storefront attempting to entice tourist to come into their shops. Above the stores, the buildings were in very poor repair and if you were sensitive to your surroundings, you could feel the underlying disquietude under the smiles and friendliness of the Cubans.

At five minutes to five, I walked into Eduardos. I looked around the room and as I did, one of the bartenders came up to me and asked in broken English, "Senor you looking for someone, or do you want to order something."

"Thank you, I'm waiting for someone."

"He looked down at my wrist and said, "Si, I know, follow me."

He led me to the back of the room, opened a door, and with a flashlight led me down a flight of stairs into a storeroom to another door. He opened it, and there sitting at a table under a lighted bulb hanging from the ceiling, was Maria. I hastily glanced around the small room that contained a few old straight- backed wooden chairs and an old, well-used, chipped porcelain topped kitchen table. Maria pointed to a chair and I sat down.

"I'm sorry for the inconvenience, but it's a necessity. May I offer you something to drink? Coffee, tea, or rum," she said.

"No thanks," I replied.

Looking at Maria, the planes on her face in the dim light and the wrinkles on her forehead reflected the years of turmoil she must have gone through. She looked at me, smiled, and asked me about Don. By her actions, I knew she was absorbing and hanging on to every word.

When I finished my tale, she smiled, covered my hand with hers, and thanked me again for bringing Don's diary to her.

"You met my father", she said," and I would love to have you meet Don's son, but in the interest of safety I cannot. After you leave this room, it is impossible to ever see or visit each other again. Maybe in the future Cuba and America will reopen contact so people can travel freely back and forth between our countries. "Quien sabe" (who knows.) I hope you understand?"

I nodded my head, "Yes Maria, I understand. Is it all right to call you Maria, or would you prefer Doctor Rodriguez?"

"Please call me Maria. I consider you part of our family after what you did and the risk you took"

She carefully, it seemed reverently, laid the diary on the table. Laying her hand on top of it, started to caress it with her fingertips as one would caress a sleeping baby.

"You mentioned yesterday about my finishing Don's diary and my story. Bringing this to me gives you every right to know. I spent all of last night reading Don's diary. I'm sure with all the tears I shed, there's many smudge marks left on its' pages."

Then, as if the thoughts going through her head had to be slowed, she placed fingers on both her temples and said, "Let me begin my story when Don left for the States. Unfortunately nothing can be recorded, otherwise it would put many people's lives in jeopardy, but I'm sure you can retain most of it."

Chapter 26

Maria's Story

When I came down to breakfast, Mamazita, Papa, and Jorge were already there waiting for me to join them. Mamazita pointed to my coffee cup under which was a note, and on my butter plate was Don's ID bracelet. Knowing he was going to leave early, and not making plans to see him, now I regret that decision. I did not realize how upset his leaving was going to affect me. I could not eat or drink anything. I put on his ID, in front of the family, folded the note into a smaller size, put it in my pocket and excused myself from the table. In my bedroom, I read his note and started to cry.

There was a knock on the door and Mamazita asked if she could come in. She came over to the bed, put her arms around me and rocked me as she did when I was a little girl.

"Mama, I know he had to leave, but it hurts so much to even think he's not here." "Maria, we will all miss him. He has a career to start and so do you. If its gods will, you will be together some time soon. I'm sure he feels as you do, so wipe your tears and let's see what the future brings."

I knew Mamazita was right but I could not stop crying. I had so many thoughts going through my head and the heaviest of feelings in my heart. I knew I could not do anything to change what had just happened and knew it best to return to the university, as soon as possible, to prepare for graduation and have all my friends around me. Once there, I would be able to put his leaving on the back burner, at least during the day.

Medical school was overwhelming but I was maintaining a straight A grade average in all my subjects. Don and I were in touch by phone and mail every week. The time we could be together was precious to both of us and we planned on meeting as often as time would allow, whether it be Miami, Matanzas, or Havana. The family knew we were going to get married; it was just a matter of my completing my schooling and internship and his new business becoming profitable.

I was sitting in one of my classes when a student came over and said I was wanted in the Medical Director's office.

"Senorita Rodriguez?" he asked as I walked in.

"Si, what can I do for you Professor?"

"I understand your family are large landowners in Matanzas, is that correct?"

"Si senor, we have been there over 300 years. Why do you ask?"

"Let me ask another question if I may," he continued. "Your brother, a former Cuban Air Force officer, has leaning towards Castro's movement?"

"I don't know anything about that, but what has all this got to do with me?"

"What a dichotomy," he said, as he looked at his desk and started to rearrange some papers." "It seems your family may be on both sides of the coin."

"One other question if I may?" Your fiancé is American and lives in the States, verdad?"(true).

"I ask you again Professor, what has all this got to do with me?"

"I'd appreciate your answer to my last question."

"Si, Don is American."

"Please sit down, Senorita. I'd like you to hear me out."

"I've been asked to go over your grades, they are exemplary. Your internship after graduation will be no problem. What discipline are you interested in?" he asked.

Without hesitation I responded, "Pediatrics."

"And why Pediatrics?" he asked.

"I feel babies deserve a good start and medical care is part of that."

"Esta bien," he said. "One other question; what do you think of Castro's proposal of healthcare if he becomes our new Presidente?"

This was now a tricky question. Castro was nowhere close to becoming president, and students were being expelled for the slightest leanings toward being pro-Fidel.

"Senor", I have no idea what Castro's plans are for healthcare, so I cannot comment, the only thing I can say with assurance is that I want to be a doctor of Pediatrics and that's the only side of politics I'm interested in."

He looked at me, smiled and said, "I have been directed to tell you that you were selected for an interview with Dr. Enrico Barca next Wednesday at 10 a.m., in Havana.

I looked at him and said, "Can you please tell me why I was chosen for this interview, or what it will be about?"

He shook his head, "Senorita, I'm just doing what I have been asked to do. I have no idea of whom, why or what is behind it, nor is it my business. All I know and have to pass on to you is that your grades are above average and you are a leader in every class you have taken. However, from what little I hear, it is my understanding that its outcome will benefit all future students in during their internship. Beyond that, I know nothing. I wish you the best of luck on your interview and hope you understand what an opportunity may be opening for you. Do you have questions?"

I was confused, I had no idea what was happening. Dr. Barca was the head of all Pediatric hospitals in Cuba. Why me? What is behind it? More important, who is behind it?

He rose from behind his desk, came around it, shook my hand and opened the office door with "Bueno Suerte" (Good luck) and closed the door behind me.

I went directly to the nearest phone and called Don at his home in New Jersey.

"Querido, listen to what just happened. Of all the students in the medical school, I have been selected for something special and it is concerning a new approach to training interns and residents here in Cuba. I have to meet with the head of Pediatrics at the hospital next week to find out more about this new concept in their training."

As the words tumbled out of my mouth, my explanation was getting jumbled even to my ears. I stopped and asked, "What do you think?"

"I think it is a great opportunity and I'm happy for you. You put your heart and soul into everything you do and I'm sure with your brain and abilities, you will do well. Have you any idea who sponsored you?" Don asked.

"No idea," I replied.

Underneath though, I was catching something in his voice that did not ring with his words or good wishes.

"Is there something wrong," I asked, "I feel there's something you want to say but do not want me to get upset. Am I wrong?"

"Maria, we never play games or hide anything, so let me ask you a question.

Didn't we agree that after you received your degree and completed your internship you'd come to the States, that we would be married, and you'd complete your residency here?"

"Yes", I replied, "but can't you see that I've been singled out for whatever reason by Dr. Barca and have an appointment with him in a few days."

"Sure," Don said, "You're absolutely right. Look, I have to go. I will call you later in the week."

We hung up. I was torn between elation and dejection. I called home and spoke to Mamazita and Papa who were delighted with the news. I knew as soon as I hung up the phone, Mama would be calling all our friends and relatives telling them of their daughter's potential new opportunity even though she knew nothing more than I did, which was very little.

CHAPTER 27

Maria looked away from the diary and continued her story.

Wednesday morning at exactly 9:45, I arrived at Dr. Barca's office. My hands were trembling; my chest felt as if someone was sitting on it, and my throat was dry, all symptoms of nervousness and anticipation. I presented myself to the receptionist and in a trembling voice said.

"I am Maria Rodriquez for my appointment with Dr. Barca."

The receptionist was an older woman, who introduced herself as Sara. She immediately attempted to put me at ease by making small talk about the weather and told me how many years she was with the doctor. I felt drawn to her as I would to my grandmother.

"Would you care for a cup of coffee or tea?" she said.

I could barely croak out a "No thank you."

"I understand you have excellent grades in Medical School," she said, again trying to ease my tension.

"I've been fortunate and enjoyed all my subjects."

"Well please make yourself comfortable, the doctor will be with you shortly."

Relax, how can I relax I thought. To keep occupied, I picked up a magazine, opened it and immediately put it down. Looked at the paintings on the wall, then at a bird sitting on a branch outside the window, doing anything to calm myself. I was just reaching a state of nirvana when I heard footsteps in the hallway approaching the door. It swung open and all the nervousness returned in full force.

I had no conception of what Dr. Barca looked like. In school, we all heard his name dozens of times and heard what a brilliant man he was. His innovative approach to pediatrics and what he accomplished over the years as the head of Pediatrics throughout the Country was well known in the medical community. When he walked in it was as if I were looking at my father's twin, tall, military bearing, tanned features, a warm smile and about Papa's age.

"Encontado, Senorita Rodriguez. It is a pleasure to meet someone so young, beautiful and intelligent," he said. I am sorry I am a few minutes late, let's go into my office for a chat."

He held the door open as I walked in, pointed to one of the chairs at a round marble tea table set for three, and asked Sara to bring in coffee and pastry for the three of us.

Making himself comfortable in one of the chairs, he explained that Sara was his right hand, knew him like a book, was indispensable, and ran his schedule like an army sergeant.

While we were waiting for Sara, I hastily glanced around the room at the furnishings, as well as the framed pictures on the walls. They showed conservative male taste and the framed pictures were all of Cuban scenes done in bright watercolors. There was not one degree nor diploma exhibited, nor a picture of Dr. Barca by himself or with anyone else.

When Sara brought in the coffee and pastry and made herself comfortable, he looked at me and said, "Tell us about yourself."

I knew he already knew everything about me, so I said, "Where should I start?"

"Well, I know about your grades, why not start at why you want to be a doctor and why Pediatrics."

Between conversation, sips of coffee, nibbles of pastry, which I ate from nervousness, an hour passed as if it were minutes. Then Dr. Barca looked at me and asked, "I understand your brother has Castro leanings, no?"

"Si", I responded.

And one other question if I may; "Your finance is American?"

"Si", I again responded.

"So tell me, Senorita Rodriguez, are you going to get married before you get your degree or after you complete your internship? Are you planning to relocate to the States?"

My mind swirled. How should I answer these questions? On one hand, I knew the plan was to finish my internship in Cuba before getting married, but do I tell him of my plans to go to the States after that?

I looked Dr. Barca straight in the eye and said, "Dr. Barca, I do not lie and I can honestly say my future plans include marrying Don, but not before finishing my internship. There is no plan to move to the States, at present.

"Maria, Cuba needs more doctors. The reason you have been invited here is to listen to a potential change I am proposing for the internship and residency requirements at all Cuban training hospitals. What we have now is antiquated, inefficient and takes too long. What I need, what I am looking for, is someone going through the present program to evaluate it while designing and implementing a new one to accomplish everything that needs to be done in a shorter period of time. Your name was submitted and approved for this position."

This was a lot of information for me to absorb. If I succeeded with this new program of Dr. Barca's, I could be responsible for major changes in the education of all future doctors. I could not believe what I was being offered. I would be a woman involved in a new training system for everyone, in the future, shortening his or her internship and residency.

My life plans and marriage were in opposition in this equation.

"Dr. Barca, I have many things to think about. For me to give you an answer at this moment is very difficult, but I am leaning toward this new proposal you are offering me. May I have a few moments to think this through?"

Dr. Barca looked at me, a very serious look, then turned and looked at Sara.

Something passed between them, and he said, "Maria, would you please wait in the reception room for a few minutes. I have some thoughts I would like to share with Sara and I can understand you are need to think about it as well. Have a cup of tea or coffee, and we both can make our decisions."

"Of course". I got up and closed the door behind me as I walked into the reception room, and tried to sort out my options.

It seemed like an eternity, not only waiting for an answer, but in the realization of what I had said to Dr. Barca. I stood as the inner door opened and they both came toward me. Sara walked over and kissed me on both cheeks. "Oh, oh, the kiss of death," I thought. Then Dr. Barca came over put out his hand on my shoulder, smiled and said, "Well Maria, what is your decision?"

"Dr. Barca, I want to be part of your team."

"Welcome Maria, we are pleased you are joining us, we were hoping you would." Upon graduation, your schedule with us will be waiting. It will be difficult completing your internship and participating in the training program but we are confident you will be able to do an outstanding job in both areas, as you have demonstrated in the past."

I could not help breaking down in front of them. All the years of studying, memorizing, writing, researching and burning the midnight oil paid off. Sara came over and put her arms around me while, through my tears, I thanked them at least a dozen times. I could not wait to find a telephone and call home to thank Mamazita and Papa for all that they had given and done for me. Then an unexpected thought popped into my head; Don and I were going to announce our wedding date to all the family at Papa's birthday party, I have some decisions to make.

That weekend I went home, threw open the door and yelled, "The future Dr. Rodriguez is here to see her Mama and Papa."

The proud look in their eyes was enough to make my heart burst, so at lunch before any relatives or friends came over, I had to sit down and go over every sentence, every word of my interview. At the end of the third telling, Papa looked at me and said, "Maria I know you work hard and spend long hours doing your studies as your marks show, but I am a bit confused. With Cuba in the turmoil it's in, not knowing if Batista will remain President or Castro will come to power, have you any idea who's behind it?"

"I have no idea why I was selected other than my grades at medical school. I really do not care who or what is behind it. It is an opportunity of a lifetime with no strings attached other than my doing well in my internship. I am as surprised as you are. Do you think I should reject it?"

"Maria, from my age and experience, time will tell. All I can suggest is play it out and see what happens. Just do not lose your dignity or self-worth for ten pieces of silver."

I was on Cloud Nine, as they say in the States, all weekend and it was Monday morning on my way to the medical school when I realized my Sunday phone call from Don never came.

We made it a point to only call each other only on Sundays so as not to interfere with business or school. Sundays we could be relaxed and talk with no pressure. Since he did not call, I was sure it was because of business, so we would speak twice as long next Sunday. When the phone rang Wednesday evening, I was surprised that it was Don.

"Querido, (Dear) what happened that you're calling today?"

"Maria, remember our conversation at the Fontainebleau about me starting my own Company?"

"Si, I remember."

"Well, I started my own business this past Monday. Mr. Ruggiero thought it was a mistake, but he gave me a sizeable bonus check and wished me well.

The construction industry seems to be expanding rapidly, which will need my product. It is a well-publicized fact that the government has started to investigate the entire olive oil industry, from importers, to bottlers, wholesalers and distributors. It does not affect me, but you know I never enjoyed working for anyone, so I figured now was the opportune time to make the change, so I did. I found a small empty factory building in New Jersey and ordered the necessary machinery, raw materials, and two people I know to do the manufacturing while I am taking care of sales. In fact, before I even open the doors, I have two large orders."

"Could Papa help financially?"

"No Querida, I saved a little and don't want to be responsible or beholding to anyone. If it works, I did the right thing, if it does not, only I will suffer. By the way, what is the family doing for Papa's birthday? Should I plan on coming down there or is the family coming to Miami?"

"The final plans have not been made. I am sure you are keeping up with the news from here so you know everything is in a state of flux."

"Hey, then I'll make plans to come down, it wouldn't be too difficult to break away for a long weekend."

With that, we hung up. No words of endearment passed between Don and me. My appointment to be involved in the new Intern/Resident Program didn't come up in our conversation either. Come to think of it, the entire conversation was like walking on broken glass by both of us.

CHAPTER 28
PAPA'S BIRTHDAY PARTY

I remembered a saying Papa used to say, "When in doubt, don't." The next Sunday when I called Don he was so pleased with what was happening in his business that I did not want to mention my perceived tension between us that I was feeling. When he finally gave me a chance to talk, I said, "The family has decided to have Papa's birthday in Matanzas, so fly down. Jorge and I will pick you up at the Matanzas airport."

"Great," he said. "I'll call you next week with the flight number and arrival time.

I can't wait to see you and hold you in my arms."

We hung up and little guilt feelings were stirring in me for not speaking up. The next Friday the semester was over. Jorge came to pick up my belongings at the school. When the truck was packed, he said, "Hey", after driving all the way from Matanzas isn't it worth your while buying me lunch and where are all the chiquitas you were going to introduce me to?"

"Dear brother, they all left for home yesterday, but I'll buy you lunch since you're going to have to listen to me. I really need to talk to someone. I have a problem and need to find a solution before Don comes down next week and I do not want Mama and Papa to know. Promise to keep it to yourself."

"Sure Maria, it's safe with me."

Jorge and I had always been close and while we bickered as all brothers and sisters do, Jorge always looked after me as a big brother. More importantly, he always listened and kept things to himself, so explaining the problem and mutually looking for solutions with Jorge was easy.

I started by telling him about my meeting with the professor at the school, even though he had heard most of it from Mama and Papa. Then I continued with my meeting with Dr. Barca, what was presented and what I said about the degree and internship being more important than getting married. We mulled everything over minutely on the drive back home. Sometimes he asked a question, sometimes we just rode in silence, thinking. Talking about it to Jorge took a tremendous weight off my chest and we both came to the same conclusion; I needed to tell Don that our future might not be as we planned.

We were so involved in our conversation that we completely forgot about lunch. Nearing the house before my brother brought up the subject in a teasing way, I said, "Jorge I didn't buy you lunch as promised, but I promise you one in the future with the prettiest girl I know." He nodded in agreement and smiled. Then I asked, "Jorge, would you mind if I picked Don up at the airport next week by myself?"

"No, Maria, I think you should," he responded.

The plane landed on time and I waited anxiously until I saw Don coming down the moveable staircase that was alongside the plane's door. When he started walking across the tarmac towards the waiting room, my heart beat faster. All the anxiety I felt disappeared. This was my love, and future husband. One day I hoped we would be married, have children, and grow old together… but now the timing was uncertain.

Being in his arms, my feelings of love, security and passion all rose up at once and I knew he felt the same. I could feel every muscle in his body pulling me to him.

"Maria, I missed you terribly," he said.

We kissed passionately in front of everyone in the waiting room and we could not let go of each other. Finally, we broke apart, looked at each other, laughed and kissed again.

"We should have met in Havana and spent the night there," Don whispered in my ear.

"Well my horney American, I'm sure we can do something about that since I have a blanket in the car, a bottle of wine and there's plenty of beautiful scenery between the airport and our home."

"Damn," he replied, "no wonder I love you."

Later, after we made love, folded the blanket and got back into the car, the night appeared even more beautiful; a full moon, not a cloud in the sky and millions of stars seemed to conspire just for us. Don knew the road as well as I did, so he drove and I just let my head rest on his shoulder while my hand rested on his thigh, he was mine and I truly loved him. When we reached the plantation, Mama, Papa and Jorge were sitting on the patio waiting for us. We had to have a few glasses of wine and tell stories of what happened since the last time we were all together.

Mamazita, in her profound wisdom, put Don in the adjoining bedroom to mine although I knew we were not fooling anyone and surprisingly, Papa, who was very conservative, did not even raise an eyebrow. Jorge, being Jorge gave me a thumb up sign, and winked when no one was looking. Finally, at 3 a.m., we all turned in since it was the day of Papa's party and we were going to celebrate it as we did a Cuban "Noche Buena," as we do on Christmas Eve with a giant pig roast.

We spent the entire morning decorating the house and cooking. We used Papa's favorite pass time, dominos, as the theme. Everything was done in black and white, with actual dominos scattered everywhere. Papa's party would start at about 4 p.m., with musicians playing bongo drums, guitars, and maracas, wearing straw sombreros. Drinks would include; mojitos, rum, beer, wine, soda, with pork rinds and banana chips to go along with them. Large platters of fruit (coconut, pineapple, sugar cane, bananas, oranges, mangos, papayas) were placed around the room. The menu would consist of; creamed plantain soup, roasted pig, coconut chicken, pork with salsa, black beans, yucca, corn fritters and for dessert, café con leche custard, flan and tres leches. The tables were so laden with food; a hurricane couldn't carry them away.

Between the uncles, aunts, sons, daughters, and grandchildren there must have been at least one hundred people present wishing Papa a happy birthday. Everyone knew and liked Don so there was no strain on his part mingling with the family. As in all parties such as this, invariably the men would drift off by themselves talking about soccer teams, politics and other manly subjects while smoking their cigars and drinking rum. The women's subjects would be children, households, gossip, and the inevitable question for me, "When are you and Don getting married?"

I still didn't have the courage to tell Don about the our change in future plans and all my decisions, I knew it was not fair or right. Living in this fantasy world of being on vacation with no pressure and him being back in Matanzas was something I didn't want to disturb but I knew I had to. Therefore, I promised myself to tell him what I told Dr. Barca tomorrow, after Papa's party.

Just after the pig was served and everyone's plate and glass was full, Papa stood up, tapped his glass with a knife, and held up his hand for everyone to be quiet.

"I want to thank everyone for being here breaking bread with us on my birthday.

Let us bow our heads and say Grace before we start to eat and thank the Good Lord for our health and this food before us. May we all have health and prosper this coming year."

Everyone bowed their heads; even the children were quiet. After Grace was said, Papa again tapped his wine glass.

"Un momento, por favor (a moment please). One other announcement that I have thought long and hard over, I feel it is in the financial interest of the family that, at my age, I retire and give the supervision of the plantation over to Jorge.

Jorge already knows the operation as well as I do, but most importantly, he has been doing business with companies outside of Cuba and has a more modern feel for world finance and international trade than I do. So a toast to our family being together and to Jorge, the new 'El Jefe' (the Chief)."

With that, everyone stood, raised their glasses to Jorge, and drank. I looked at my brother Jorge and realized he was as surprised as everyone else and I was happy for him. It was time for Papa to start taking it easy. I looked at Don, held his hand and our lips touched. My family was all around me with the security only a loving family can give.

Then Jorge stood up and wanted everyone to know he appreciated Papa's offer but wanted to speak to Papa alone before accepting. This came as a complete surprise to everyone and for some reason I started to feel a little uneasy. Maybe this was just the excuse I needed to tell Don that this was not the right time to tell everyone about our wedding plans. I had to tell Don everything. I leaned over and whispered to him that we needed to have a serious discussion about the future, and perhaps this was not the time to make any announcement of our own. He looked at me for a long time, nodded and said in a flat tone of voice, "Maybe you're right."

One thing we both noticed though, after dinner Papa and Mamazita spent an unusual amount of time with Rafael's parents in Papa's study, but only later found out what is was about. After they left, Papa and Jorge were out on the patio for some time talking, and from what little I heard it was a very serious conversation. Then I heard Papa say he was tired and they would continue talking in the morning. At breakfast, Jorge announced that he was giving control of the Plantation back to Papa and in a few days, he would be with Castro. Nothing any of us said could change his mind.

Jorge's decision was upsetting enough but this was compounded by my mind conjuring up various ways to tell Don what happened in Dr. Barca's office and explain it in a logical manner he would understand. Unfortunately, my putting it off until tomorrow had arrived; tomorrow was now today.

"What do you want to do today?" I asked Don.

"Well, other than wanting to make love to you, let's take a car and just drive along the ocean, and get away from people."

"Sounds good to me, I'll fix a basket so we needn't come home until dinnertime."

We found a little cove on a sandy beach, laid out a blanket and watched at the small waves breaking on the shore. Puffy little white clouds were building into rain clouds and I'll never forget, the thought crossing my mind that maybe this was an omen of things to come.

"Maria", Don said, "You have something on your mind. What's bothering you?"

With that I touched my fingers to his ID bracelet that I wore constantly, said a small prayer and it all poured out. An hour later I was completely empty, everything was out in the open and I felt better since I never again wanted anything unspoken or hidden between us.

Don poured wine for both of us, looked at me, looked at the ocean, and said, "Maria since I've known you, I have loved you. I know how hard you studied and proud you are working on your medical degree. You have a tremendous opportunity offered to you and if you did not take it, sometime in the future you may wish you had, so I will not stand in your way. My business has started off great, and I'm getting more work than I know what to do with. Surprisingly, I don't know where it's coming from any more than you know where your offer came from. We can see each other every few weeks, so another year or two to get where we want to be career wise isn't too long a time. We also do not know what is happening here in Cuba. When things quiet down, I would love to sell the business and come back here, or by that time, you may want to come north. Let's leave the future to the future. The main thing is that we will be married one day; in fact I already feel we are, so rest your pretty head on my chest and let me hold you close before we go back. All that matters is I love you, and you love me."

I turned into him. He understood. I was so lucky Jorge brought him into our family.

We spent the rest of the vacation, visiting friends and relatives, even spent a night at Aunt Clara's house in Havana and, like every dream, it ended with Don going back to the States and me to the hospital to begin my internship and new assignment.

Months after Papa's birthday party, Mamazita received a letter from Jorge saying everything was fine, he was in good health and thought he would be in Havana by the end of the year and hopefully spend New Year's Eve, with the family. It was never meant to be. Jorge never showed up.

I was putting in eighteen hours a day, with half days on weekends. There was no opportunity to relax. Don and I spoke every weekend and every weekend I called home to see how the family was.

Christmas was rapidly approaching and though it was extremely difficult, Don managed to get his visa renewed. The biggest surprise was the week before Don arrived.

Aunt Clara called me and asked if we could meet for lunch. We met at a local restaurant and she seemed a bit uneasy. She kept stammering and making innocuous small talk about nothing. Finally I said, "Aunt Clara, can you please tell me what's troubling you, you are driving me crazy."

She stammered, blushed, sipped some coffee and said, "Maria, please don't think badly of me, forward, or intrusive, but Mama and I have been speaking and I'd like you and Don to stay at my house, since you'll both be in Havana. Your parents and I are planning to spend a few days at your cousin, Carlos', house in Marianao and the house will be empty. I understand Don will be here for only a short time and so why should you be with us old people? All the nightlife, what is left of it and young people are here in Havana, plus my house is sitting empty. Why don't you and Don stay there? In that way you'll be free to do and go anywhere in Havana you wish without worrying about money for hotels or feeling obligated to be around your parents."

I was speechless! My conservative Aunt Clara and my mother speaking and agreeing on something as monumental as this. I reached across the table, held her hand in mine and looked into her eyes and saw the love. I could not help but get up from my chair, walk around to her, put my arm around her shoulders, and kiss her.

"Thanks, Aunt Clara, from both of us."

"Good" she said, "now let's order something, I'm starved."

Don being here, and Christmas, it was hectic, but Don and I spent every moment we could with each other. Staying by ourselves in Aunt Clara's house, in the city was certainly a plus. It was playing house for the few days before Don went back to the States. We had an entire house to ourselves, to make love in any room we chose, to get up any time we wished, to go to any show or eat in any restaurant we wanted to. Most importantly, to hold hands walking along the streets or along the Malecon, to watch the waves breaking over the seawall and listen to the strolling guitarists. To be totally immersed only in each other. We were oblivious to anyone or anything around us.

Over Christmas, seemingly by unspoken mutual consent, we did not bring up the subject of marriage so thankfully, it did not disrupt our time together. His business was doing well, but things in Cuba were chaotic and seemed to be in a downward spiral.

Unfortunately, we could not help comparing this Christmas in Aunt Clara's house to last Christmas on the plantation. As conservative as Aunt Clara and my parents are, they were kind enough to give Don and me plenty of time to be alone, for which I thanked them for.

Don flew back to New Jersey the next day.

Relations between the United States and Cuba, since Castro took power, steadily deteriorated. American presents on the Island was solely Guantanamo Bay, the military naval base. With Castro concerned about an invasion by U.S. forces, he allowed Russian troops and naval forces to begin establishing military bases on Cuban soil. Contracts were signed to trade Cuban sugar for Russian oil and other goods. Little by little, the Russians started to take control over some Cuban government departments. The Russians goal was to change all of Cuba's political and financial aspects of government to resemble their own, a total police state. No Cuban was allowed an exit Visa, and American travelers, while welcomed for their dollars, were few and far between and looked on suspiciously. Shortly thereafter all diplomatic, tourists, mail, and telephone communications were cut-off between Cuba and the United States.

Many times, I thought about life and the decisions we make. Because of me, our dream of marriage was now delayed. Because of my decision to remain in Cuba, our plans had gone up in smoke and we may never see each other again. How can I get in touch with Don, or he with me? I kept thinking the same thoughts over and over. There seemed to be no solution to my dilemma and I ended up every thought with the same question mark. What to do or what the future might hold. As Dr. Barca once said, "Throw yourself into work and let the future take care of itself."

I completed medical school and started my internship and participation in the new program.

CHAPTER 29
MARIA (CONT.)

There's an old wives' tale that things, whether good or bad happen in three's. I always chalked it up to superstition, but sometime one has doubts.

Sitting in my temporary office in the hospital going over some medical reports when the phone rang.

"Ola, Maria Rodríguez here."

"Maria, this is Aunt Clara, you have to come here immediately."

"Aunt Clara, can it wait until this evening?"

"No, it's something bad and I can't say on the telephone."

"I'm in the middle of something important, can't it wait?"

"Maria, come here immediately," and she hung up.

I never knew Aunt Clara to be anything but calm in any emergency, so I called my supervisor and told her I had an emergency phone call and could she please cover for me for the rest of the day. She agreed, and I caught a taxi with my mind racing over every scenario I could possibly think of. It didn't take long to get there. I knocked on the door of Aunt Clara's house. Without looking to see who it was, Aunt Clara opened the door, and there sitting in a chair was Mamazita sobbing and talking hysterically.

"Mamazita, what's happened? What's wrong? Is Papa hurt?" I knelt on the floor with my arms around her. "Please tell me what's wrong."

She took the tissue away from her eyes, put her arms around me and said, "Papa is in jail."

"In jail, for what?"

"They came to take over the plantation and when Papa said they couldn't, he raised his fist to one of them. They beat him and took him to jail. No one can see him."

"Who took the plantation?"

"Some men who said they were from Castro's government and they were going to divide it up among Cubans since the land belongs to everyone. Then they told us we had to be out by the next day. Papa told them we have been there for over 300 years and that Jorge was with Castro, but it made no difference. Papa demanded some identification and they said they did not need to show it to him, but they were from the newly formed Agricultural department. One thing led to another and Papa became so angry he raised his fist to hit one of them. They all jumped on him and knocked him to the floor. When they pulled him up, his head was bleeding. His wrists were tied behind his back and they dragged Papa out of the house and pushed him into their car. I asked them where they were taking him and their only response was, "Be out of this house by tomorrow night." They would not even allow me to go near the car to kiss Papa. I started packing as many possessions as I could get into our luggage and had Jose drive me here to Clara. Maria what can we do?"

As Mamazita was telling the story, I was thinking of someone who could possibly help us. The only name that came to mind, who may know someone in a position of power was Dr. Barca. I immediately called his office and who answered but Sara.

"Sara, is Dr. Barca free tomorrow in the morning. I need to see him. It is of extreme importance and I need to speak to him concerning a personal problem."

Sara checked her appointment book and said he could meet with me at eleven. She asked if she could be of help. I thanked her but said I could not tell her what it was about over the phone. With the thought of Papa in prison, trying to comfort Mama and Aunt Clara and thinking whom, other than Dr. Barca to contact, to help. Any sleep that night was impossible.

Early the next morning, I walked into the reception room where Dr. Barca and Sara waited for me.

"Maria, it's a pleasure to see you so early in the day, Que pasa?"

"Dr. Barca, this has nothing to do with business, it's strictly personal, and I don't know if you can help or not."

"Diga me. Que es la problema?" (Tell me. What is the problem?)

Sara and I had developed a close relationship since I joined the team, so her being there wasn't embarrassing or uncomfortable. I continued, "My Papa is in prison," I blurted. "My parents were forcibly evicted from our home, my father resisted and they threw him in prison. I don't know where or who to turn to and the only one I know who may have any influence is you. Is there anyone you know who can help me? I'm so upset that I can't work or even think straight."

Dr. Barca looked at me, and then looked at Sara. He walked close, put his hand on my shoulder and said, "Let me see what I can do. That is all I can promise. Your being upset is not helping your Papa any. Get involved in work. Time will pass faster and who knows what may happen."

With that, he dismissed me with a wave of his hand. I turned, thanked them both, and went to my office.

Weeks passed and still no word about Papa. Poor Mama was aging rapidly. How could any government be as cruel and heartless as to refuse the family knowledge of where their loved ones were being held or deny permission to visit them? I did not want to annoy Dr. Barca, but I was on the telephone with Sara frequently to see if she had any news.

CHAPTER 30

On a day I shall never forget, while sitting in my office daydreaming of what might have been, looking at the fleecy white
clouds drifting past the window feeling the tension from the turmoil surrounding my life. The windows were open with the cur-
tains drifting back and forth with the light sea breeze. Hospital
voices and sounds in the background were not adding anything
peaceful or serene to my state of mind. A multitude of thoughts
were fleeting through my head, each one pushing itself in, staying awhile, then being pushed out by another. Adding to the
stress and tension, I suddenly felt queasy and I needed to throw
up. As I rushed to the bathroom my first reaction was that, I was
either sick or pregnant. Deep down I knew exactly what it was. I
was not sick!

I was in the bathroom for quite some time and knew I had
to validate my suspicion of being pregnant. If I am, how do I
get word to Don? Do I tell my parents? Do I tell Dr. Barca? Do
I abort? No, that is out of the question. I want our baby! Calm
down, I told myself, wash your face and put on fresh makeup,
relax and think things through slowly before you go to Aunt
Clara's tonight. By force of habit, I rubbed Don's ID bracelet
knowing that everything would turn out all right.

It was useless; I needed to speak to someone, someone that I respected and someone that could give me guidance, someone who was here, close, and immediate. That someone could only be Sara. My analytical medical demeanor disappeared. I was a woman needing help, needing direction, needing something.

Without knocking, I opened their office door. Sara looked at me in alarm.

"Maria, que pasa, you look terrible."

"Sara, I need to talk to you, and need your guidance."

"For you, of course, can I get you anything?"

"No, No. I need to talk to you."

"Maria, what's wrong?"

"Sara I think I'm pregnant. "

"Maria, take deep breaths, everything will be all right. The first thing you have to do is have a pregnancy test."

We arranged for the test to be done that afternoon. I felt better sharing the weight of possibly being pregnant with someone I felt close to. As I walked to my appointment, I did not feel alone or frightened only hoping, then not hoping, what the results would show. What a difference from seeing and treating women who are pregnant and now possibly experiencing pregnancy myself. ! Me, a mother! How incredible! How frightening! How wonderful!

That evening when I came home, I begged off having dinner with the family and went directly to my room saying that I had a headache. Aunt Clara wanted to bring something up to my room and Mamazita kept popping in saying I was working too hard. The thought of food turned my stomach and I just wanted the night to be over and to get the results of my test tomorrow.

I could not sleep and before any one awoke, I quietly slipped out of the house and went to my office. No sooner did I get there than the phone rang, it was Sara calling with the results of the test. I was pregnant!!

I left my office and felt the need for fresh air, sunshine and not the feeling of being hemmed in by a concrete building. I walked for a few blocks and realized I was outside the oldest church in Havana, the Inglesia del Espiritu Santo, my childhood church and my family's sanctuary for comfort and spiritual guidance for generations. Was this a sign? Science does not believe in signs! Coincidence? I felt more comfortable with that. I had not been in a church since I was in my teens, but it drew me as if an oasis would a caravan on the desert. The thought of a baby being formed inside me because of our love was overwhelming but the feelings were impossible to put into words.

However, I was never religious, walking through the church doors as my ancestors had done since the 1600s seemed to quiet my emotions. The fountain holding the holy water was in the same place as it was when I was a child. The organist was playing something of Bach. Peace and solitude settled around me like an old familiar shawl as I settled in a well-worn pew, as hundreds did before me. I reached out and rubbed my hand over the backrest of the pew in front of me. If it could only talk of the hundreds of hands that had touched that same piece of wood. How many thousands over the past 500 years had poured their hearts out silently while sitting here or in one of the confessionals? How many came here, as I did, to absorb the feeling of serenity, to find answers to their problems in quiet reflection?

Subconsciously, I pulled the kneeling bench out from under the pew in front of me.

All the prayers that were drummed into my head as a child, that were just words at the time, now started to flow through my mind with new meaning.

With all the feelings of peace and serenity, I was experiencing, realism kept intruding into my thoughts. Would my child ever know his father? How could I get word to Don? Would my pregnancy be easy? How should I tell my parents? How long would I be able to work? Who would take care of the baby if I work after it is born? Would I be forced to put the baby into a State run nursery while I am working, or would I be allowed to get private help?

Thinking these thoughts was getting me more and more upset. Then it dawned on me that I could only solve one problem at a time. I remained seated still trying to recapture the peacefulness and quiet I found when I first walked in. It was impossible!

After taking deep breaths, after trying to clear my mind of doubts and questions, the tranquility I was seeking, the answers I needed, were gone. I had to deal with all my problem head on. I arose, crossed myself, and went to break the news to my family.

Walking to Aunt Clara's house, I thought of all the things I could say, and how I could say them, knowing full well when it came time, I'd just forget it all and that's exactly what happened. As soon as I opened the door, Mamazita and Aunt Clara were surprised that I was home at this time of day. I asked if they would all gather in the living room since I had something important to tell them. I started off with, "Don and I have known each other for 4 years. If it wasn't for my wanting to be a doctor, we would have been married a year ago." They just looked at me as I continued, "Something happened today that I want you to know. I believe, in fact I'm sure," as I looked at my parents, "you're going to have a grandchild, and Aunt Clara, you will be a great-aunt." The room was quiet. The silence was deafening.

They did not say anything and the look on their faces was such that I could tell they did not absorb what I had told them. After a few seconds of silence, Mama and Aunt Clara screamed and ran to hug me. For the first time in minutes, I took a deep breath. I knew everything would be all right.

After dinner Mama and Aunt Clara wouldn't let me do any cleaning up and chatted about all the children in the family and if there were twins and, if so, on who's side.

The next day, I requested an appointment with Dr. Barca, and explained to Sara that I had told my parents and would now like to tell Dr. Barca. The three of us were again sitting at the small table we sat around at my first interview. Glancing around I noticed the ash tray I had given him sitting in a prominent position on his desk, which pleased me, and when he looked in my direction, he said, "So my dear, why the big smile?"

"Dr. Barca, I'm pregnant!"

"Wonderful! Have you told your parents, and I presume it is the American's child?"

"Yes and yes," I replied.

"Sara and I are happy for you and this takes us back to the conversation we had over a year ago if you recall."

"Si Professor."

"So what are your future plans, if I may ask?"

"I truthfully don't know, but realistically, since it's impossible to leave Cuba, all my energies are here. Whether the baby will ever know or be held by his father is up to fate or diplomacy."

"Well, Maria, let me tell you this. The people that are in charge of the Cuban Health Program know all about what you are doing in our Internship Program.

Another Country, namely Russia, is taking your experiences and introducing them to the Soviet bloc nations it oversees. Because of this, you may become an international celebrity in your field. Your being pregnant has no bearing on what you could accomplish whether here, in the States or anywhere else in the world. Whatever you decide is your decision, and I wish you well no matter what it is, though at this time you're limited as to where you can go."

All the while Sara was sitting and nodding affirmatively to everything he was saying. He rose from his chair, opened a wood panel in the wall that concealed a refrigerator, reached in and brought out a bottle of Champagne. Pouring into three glasses, he said, "To our Maria and our baby, saluda, dinero y amor." (Health, wealth and happiness).

The first person to know I was pregnant should have been Don, but getting a phone call or a letter to the States was impossible. No incoming mail was distributed and outgoing mail to the States was prohibited. Phone lines as well as telegraph lines were cut.

Anyone listening to American radio stations was immediately thrown into prison. Martial Law was declared. It was now illegal for any Cuban to leave the Country or to trade with. the United States. My baby would be born without his or her father at my side.

Americans have a slogan I admire, "Turn a lemon into lemonade" and that I did. I threw myself into my work, which entailed working with the Cuban Health Group as well as the Russian

Group and representatives from other South and Central American countries. We even had a small group from China interested in our training program as well as several countries in Africa.

I was so busy, the months flew by and I had an uneventful pregnancy. After opening my office door that day, I walked to the window and had a premonition that today was the day I was going to give birth. I felt I could encompass all the beauty of the morning into my outstretched arms. The birds were singing, and the leaves of the palm trees were lazily waving back and forth. Clouds were starting to build over the sea, and a slight breeze was coming in off the Straits with the slight tang of salt. What a glorious, magnificent day to bring my baby into the world. All of a sudden, I felt the first pain in my abdomen. I was right about the day and I knew what was going to happen. My first thought was my wish that Don was here with me but since that was impossible; I had to go through it by myself.

My first call was to Mamazita. Between her going into every detail, asking endless questions, then repeating it to Aunt Clara, I had to tell her I was going to have her grandchild speaking to her on the telephone if she didn't hang up. My second call was to Sara, telling her I was on my way down to the maternity floor and to please inform Dr. Barca.

A nurse I knew well, helped me after I was admitted and stayed with me for the next few hours while I went through the stages of labor. At times I could swear I heard my mother yelling outside the delivery room that she wanted to be with me since she had been a midwife for many women. This was news to me, as she had never mentioned anything about her ever being a midwife and someday I thought, I would have to ask her about it.

Nine hours later the nurse laid a beautiful eight-pound boy in my arms. Here was my Eduardo. The tears rolled down my cheeks thinking of what Don had missed, and what I missed by not having him at my side. Only then did I start counting my baby's fingers and toes to make sure they were all there.

Due to the position I held with the hospital, the government offered me housing and a full time nurse for the baby, but Mama and Aunt Clara needed someone to take care of and fuss over.

They would not allow anyone to take care of the baby other than themselves and only in Aunt Clara's house. Knowing that he was safe and well looked after I felt at ease and could now perform my job responsibilities. Not only was I working on the new program but also had the opportunity to learn and practice pediatric surgery, as well as giving lectures to students of many nations. Thoughts of Don and dreams of being together as a family always remained in the back of my mind.

CHAPTER 31

It was somewhere around this time that Jorge was stationed nearby. He came to Aunt Clara's house and he was not the happy–go-lucky Jorge we knew. He lost a tremendous amount of weight, was exhausted but most of all angry at how things in Cuba were going. In fact, it was the first time he and I ever had an argument and the first time he met his nephew Eduardo. As brothers and sisters do, we made up and he told us he had a new assignment crop dusting or dropping insecticides, I do not recall which but it was somewhere near or around our Plantation in Mantanzas, that was the last we heard from him.

Then one day I received a call from Dr. Barca. Papa was all right. He was being held in a place near Moro Castle, at the harbor.

Dr. Barca was allowed to see him and determined that while Papa had lost weight, he was in good health. The charge against him was for attacking a representatives of the government, not for anti-government actions, and he thought that Papa would be released shortly.

A few days later, I received a phone call at Aunt Clara's to pick Papa up at the local police station where he was now held. When I picked him up, he looked as if he had aged twenty years but held himself as erect as ever. To his credit, Papa's spirit and demeanor were still that of the "El Jefe" of old. We were not living on our plantation, but other than Jorge and Don, what was left of our family would again be together in Aunt Clara's house, with the new addition, Eduardo, to the family. I was a bit concerned how Papa would react to his grandson, but as soon as Eduardo took hold of Papa's index finger and the look on Papa's face, I knew everything would be all right.

No one could imagine the thanks I felt for what Dr. Barca had done. I bought him a beautiful crystal ashtray, but he kept denying he did anything worth this gift.

Papa was safe for the time being, but it crossed my mind that Papa was right; the opportunity I was offered was under Batista's regime, and the release of Papa yesterday was under Castro. Who was the angel sitting on my shoulder?

The rest of the year flew by. There was no opportunity to relax, but I did notice the changes that were taking place in Cuba. Businesses were closing down, the peso was devalued, inflation was rampant, and dictatorial powers were being imposed. Free speech was forbidden as well as any dissident talk against Castro's government. People were going hungry. Fidel declared Cuba an atheist country. Christmas was forbidden, since December was harvest time for sugar and that took precedent over any religious holiday. All available work forces were pressed into the fields. More and more Russian soldiers were on our streets and more and more foreigners were in our hotels.

After nearly a year of hands-on experience dealing with children, my choice of Pediatrics was the right one. I knew it was what I wanted to do the rest of my life. My internship was really the only thing that I had been concerned about for the last few years.

Things were going comparatively well. Eduardo was in excellent health, the family was together and work was a pleasure, but nothing in life runs smoothly for too long. Then the THIRD shoe fell ! After a long day at work and looking forward to seeing Eduardo, I came home to find Mamazita, Papa and Aunt Clara very agitated. Mama went on to tell me that two men from the government had come to the house that afternoon asking questions about Jorge. When was the last time we saw him? Where was he working? Who were his friends? Did we know where he goes and with whom? When does he visit us? Of course, we told then all we knew, which really was not much, since Jorge had become very quiet since he left the Army. We asked them why they were asking all these questions since we were sure they knew where he worked and had access to his records. All they said was that they were on official business and couldn't say. Then the block captain, the old man that lives at the end house down the street, kept passing the house after they left, finally knocked on the door saying that he has the right as block captain to come into our house anytime he wishes to see who is there and why. Papa rose from his chair, and was ready to throw him out.

Police cars, which we never saw before, now passed every few hours during the day, slowing down, as they went by our house. In addition, every once in a while, rather than a police car, a military car would takes its place.

This was very upsetting to all of us, so the next day while at work and away from the house, I called the air strip every chance I had. I would ask to speak to Jorge and the response was always the same, "He's flying," or "He isn't here." The people taking the calls were very courteous, always taking my phone number and saying they would give him the message to call back, but Jorge never did. That behavior was so unlike Jorge, who was always a responsible person.

A few days later, there was a knock on my office door and, unannounced two men walked in. They showed me I.D. cards from the government and asked me the same questions they asked Mamazita at home. I asked them why they wanted to know about Jorge since all his military records were available, as well as, his time with Castro. With everyone knowing where Jorge worked, why not ask him these questions directly. They looked at me coldly saying only that it was, "government business," to every question I asked. It was only later I found out, these same people had told the workers at the airstrip, not to give any information to anyone especially Jorge's family, upon penalty of prison.

Jorge, being Jorge, we knew he would call or drop in eventually when he could or was able to. Then one morning when I opened the house door to go to work, a slip of paper fell to the ground between the house door and the locked iron gate. I picked it up, read it and rushed back into the house to wake Mama, Papa and Aunt Clara. All it said was Jorge was safe in the States.

That amazing brother of mine must have done exactly as he said he was going to do the last time he was here. He stole a plane and made it safely across to Florida. It dawned on me that the last time he and I were alone I gave him Don's telephone number. Maybe, just maybe, they will be together. Maybe, he will tell Don about our son, little Eduardito.

One evening, a few months later, after walking from the hospital to Aunt Clara's house, I immediately had a bad feeling when I saw an ambulance parked in front of her house with its emergency lights flashing and a military vehicle parked there. My first thoughts were that the baby was hurt, or Papa had a heart attack, so I started to run, pushing the gawkers aside like bowling pins. The front door was wide opened and there on the floor, stretched out, was Mamazita with someone bent over her giving her oxygen.

"What happened?" I screamed at Papa. "What happened?" "Is the baby all right?"

Both he and Aunt Clara were crying.

"What happened?" I screamed again.

Papa came over and put his arms around me, tears streaming down his face. It was the first time I ever saw Papa cry. The first time I saw how much he had aged.

"Maria, we were just notified that Jorge and Rafael were killed bringing a boat load of guns into Cuba for the anti-Castro forces. When Mama heard it, she had a heart attack. It seems there was a third person in the boat but somehow they could not find him."

I knew immediately who the third person was.

I took charge and rode with Papa in the ambulance to the hospital, where we both sat in the waiting room until the doctor came out and said Mamazita was resting comfortably and suggested we go home, get some rest, and come back in the morning.

Going back to Aunt Clara's, we were both deep in our own thoughts. Poor Jorge, poor Rafael, poor Mamazita. The strain of the news was just too much for me, I could not cry anymore. I knew it would take a lot but I must find out where Jorge and Rafael were buried and I wonder who will notify Rafael's family and how, since they are in the States. Damn politics interfering in people's lives, causing disruption and hardship. If it's not about money, it is about power, and the sad part is that everyone goes out with what they came into life with nothing.

Aunt Clara was waiting for us and we told her what happened.

"Maria please, can I go back to the hospital with you and Papa?"

"Of course, I responded."

After all, Clara was her older sister and a good sister at that, for taking in the remnants of our family and making sure we were as comfortable as she could.

Next morning when we returned to the hospital there was a priest in Mama's room giving Mama last rites. This was not supposed to be. We were told she was resting comfortably when we left, and now a priest? He finished his prayers, nodded to us and left the room. Papa held her hand, kissed her on the forehead and said something in her ear. Mama smiled, looked at us, closed her eyes and passed away. Mamazita, dear, sweet Mamazita was gone.

Damn Don! No one has to tell me but I know he was with Jorge and Rafael when they died and I can indirectly blame him for Mamazita's death, but what's done is done and placing blame without facts, or making snap judgments, isn't fair either.

Eduardo was two years old when the Cuban Government gave back our Hacienda in Matanzas for the work I did and am still doing. The plantation is still sub- divided into small farms and the feeling of belonging are not the same as before, but when I am home on weekends, Papa, Eduardo, Aunt Clara and I can sit in the evenings and look to the north at the Straits of Florida and dream of what was.

Every so often, I think about life and the twists and turns it has taken. My mind drifts back to when it all started with Jorge bringing home an American who I fell in love with and who gave me a beautiful, golden-haired, blue-eyed son and the cost it brought to all of us. On the other side of the scale of life is the mysterious benefactor who gave me the opportunity to accomplish what I have, and who kept us comparatively untouched by the troubled waters around us.

CHAPTER 32

Then a year or so later, sitting at my desk in the hospital, staring at the sky, as I always do when I am stressed, when the phone rang.

"Dr. Rodriguez please."

"This is Dr. Rodriguez."

"Please hold for Dr. Barca."

"Ola, Maria. How are you, the family, and Eduardo?"

"Very well, Dr. Barca, and I apologize to you and Sara for not being in touch more often but the last few weeks have been quite hectic here."

"No problem, Maria. The reason I called is that I received a call from the Ministry of Health. It seems they had a request from the Canadian Health Minister wanting to send a representative to Cuba to compare Health Care systems. Naturally I suggested you, since you're the best we have and speak English fluently."

"Dr. Barca, I'm honored and flattered!"

"When is he or she expected?"

"I have no idea but you'll be getting a call from the Minister of Health's office giving you all the specifics in a few days. I expect it will be in a week or so. Answer all of his or her questions. Good or bad, we have nothing to hide. Stay well, and my regards to your Papa and Aunt Clara."

With that, he said goodbye and hung up.

The palm leaves were idly moving in the breeze but now a few rain clouds started to form. I felt a little uneasy and hoped that this was not a sign of things to come. What a peculiar, superstitious, silly thought to cross my mind, so unlike me.

How exciting! Someone is coming from the Free World who has the freedom to talk about anything and everything. Maybe it will be a woman and for the first time in years I can talk about woman's fashions and at least mentally to get out of this white medical coat.

Who am I kidding, free speech in Cuba! I find I'm even now starting to censor my own thoughts and watching my every word for fear of it being misinterpreted by someone.

Will the laws ever change whereby Cubans and American will be able to visit each other's country again? Will Don, Eduardo and I will ever be together as a family, whether in Cuba or the States? What would it be like to live in a free Country? Would I give up everything here and move to the States to marry Don, without question! I put myself and *my* wants above *our* wants and have been paying for it ever since. I could be living there where you do not have to stand in line for food. Where children are well fed, and loved by parents who could tuck them in at night rather than sending them to government schools where the State is more important than the parents. Where children that can get a well-rounded education, with subjects not rewritten by any Minister of Education, and where they can travel anywhere without an I.D. card or needing to request permission from a government agency. Where the ill can have the treatment they need in a reasonable length of time, medicines are readily available, and people do not live in fear of being singled out as anti- government and thrown into prison, or worse.

What would it would feel like to visit neighbors, have coffee, and not worry about block captains barging in, or microphones listening to every word, where everyone could again, be as happy as they choose to be and take any path in life they choose. Will Cuba ever be like this again?

My daydream continued, I pictured the person coming was Don. He was arranging, through a neutral country to take me back to the States. Then reality set in, how selfish on my part. Under the Cuban policy, the defector could possibly leave, but no other family member could. Everything the defector and their immediate family owned would be confiscated by the State. Therefore, Eduardo, Papa and Aunt Clara would have to stay and lose everything and go on charity. In all probability Eduardo would be an outcast, humiliated the rest of his life by peer pressure, constantly being watched as if he were a criminal and immediately dropped from school. Papa would be put back in jail, and Aunt Clara would be placed in some institution. They would be purposely separated from each other forever, with no contact allowed. It is the same dictatorial reason that an emissaries of Cuba, sent to foreign countries are not allowed to take family members with them. The family members, friends and co-workers here are all held under strict surveillance until the emissary returns. That alone would be too big a price to pay for my freedom, never mind all the children and patients I am responsible for. That thought snapped me fully awake. If Don and I were ever to meet again, or if there was any way we could communicate in the future, it would be best for him and his future if I said Eduardo was not his child and blame him for Jorge's and Mama's deaths whether he was with Jorge or not. My rational being Don would think I was taking the Castro line of propaganda, blaming all Americans for Cuba's and our family's problems. Realistically it looks like I will never have to take this stand and it may be decades before we could possibly be together, if ever. I wish with all my heart and love he starts a new life in the States without us. It would break my heart but it is the best solution for all. I wonder if I have the courage to do it, if we ever met. . As you sow, so shall ye reap. My mistake! My punishment! My thoughts are getting me more and more agitated. Enough philosophizing, I had better shake myself from this introspective mood, get back to work and keep my mind occupied in the here and now. There is no time for crying and my decision has been made.

Another week flew by when my receptionist received a call from a Mr. Belmont, from the Canadian government who was at the Hotel National, requesting an appointment for the next morning at 10 a.m. She asked me if I was available at that time and I agreed. Unfortunately, it was a Mr. Belmont not a Miss or Mrs.

The next morning at 10 a.m., Mr. Belmont was at the receptionist desk to interview me about Pediatric Health Care in Cuba.

"Please send Mr. Belmont in."

I heard the footsteps of the receptionist walking down the tiled hallway with the visitor. She knocked, opened the door and announced, "Dr. Rodriguez, Mr. Belmont from Canada is here for his 10 o'clock appointment."

I stood up to greet him and to welcome him to Cuba. I thought it most odd that he was wearing dark sunglasses indoors, and the thought crossed my mind it was peculiar that as soon as he entered the room he turned and closed the door. He turned to me, removed the glasses and my brain could not accept what I was seeing. Was it really Don?

I vaguely remember stepping around my desk, with one hand on it to steady myself and the back of my other hand accidently hit Eduardo's framed photograph, knocking it onto the floor. I looked down at the broken glass with the bent frame and the photo of Eduardo facing up, strange how you remember the weirdest things. To this day I remember saying to myself how difficult it will be to clean up all the broken glass from the frame.

Don looked down at the photo then looked up at me. My jumbled thoughts were starting to stabilize and putting facts together. It was Don! He opened his arms to embrace me.

"Si Querida, it's me." (Yes, dearest, it is me)

I took a step towards him. I wanted to be in his arms as much as he wanted me there.

Then I stopped. The cold bucket of reality dumped upon me. My thoughts of only a half hour or so came rushing through my brain. I could not leave Cuba and Don could not come back here. I had a life and family here and for his future had to cut our ties so, he could start his life in the States. I put my hand on his chest and pushed him away.

I could feel his heart beating through his shirt. I had to do what I had to do now or I would crumble.

The throbbing in my temple started as it always did when I was upset. I backed away, lifted my right hand, pointed, and said, "Murderer, how dare you come here after killing my brother and as a result of that, my mother also. We welcomed you into our family, into our home, I welcomed you into my arms and death is the thanks you gave in return."

Don face turned ashen.

"Maria, it's me. It's Don."

"I know very well who you are, a murderer, I want nothing to do with you."

Then he started telling me how he risked his life coming here and I cut him off by saying the cruelest thing.

"I'll be happy when you're dead like Jorge, Mamazita and Rafael are."

I am sure there was more, but I was spouting threats and I truthfully do not remember all the hurtfully things I said to him or the scorn, insults and threats I directed his way. My heart was breaking but it was something that had to be done. By this time, Don's face was a mask of hurt, anger and disbelief. He looked at me, turned and walked out. I accomplished what I set out to do, turning him against me.

When I purposely slammed the door after Don, it was slamming the door on both our lives. Don, all his dreams shattered, now was forced to go on to a new life, and me, loving him as much as I do, to an empty existence.

Glass was all over the floor. I gently picked up the photo of Eduardo and placed it on my desk. Then the craziest vision popped into my head. Something I have not thought about since I was a little girl. Our family was visiting cousins in Spain and for, the first time in my life, I went to the bullfights. When this magnificent bull entered the ring, the picadors on horseback tormented him with lances to tire him, to bleed him out before the matador did the "coup de grace". That is what I just did, tortured

Don, tormented him, giving him a slow death, but there is no matador to cleanly give him or me closure. What I did was right but the realization of his leaving forever that was killing me. My head was reeling. I ran to the restroom and kept washing my face until someone happened to come in and asked me if I was all right, I nodded my head since I could not find my voice. Then, back at my desk, I called the Administrator telling him I had to go back to Matanzas for a few days. If I stayed in Havana, I knew I would end up at the Nacional, only prolonging the agony of what had to be. I desperately needed to be in a place far from Havana until he flew out. I needed a place surrounded by people I loved, that loved me back and could give me the feeling of security I needed now; that place was the plantation surrounded by a loving family.

Maria wiped the tears from her eyes and the tears rolling down her cheeks.

"Please forgive me", she said," I took the wrong turn in the road and everyone suffered and now, now it's too late to change anything."

I was silent while she gathered herself.

"Well my dear American friends, you now have the end of the story and to answer your question before you ask, I never did tell Don that Eduardo was his son."

She stood and placed her hand on my arm, and said, "One unanswered question, I'm sure has crossed your mind, is who was behind all the events in my families lives; my education, where I am today, and how did we get the business above us, as she lifted her arm and pointed to the store above, or for that matter, our return to the hacienda? We have never lost our dignity, never caused problems, and always tried to help everyone we could. We have been extremely fortunate, much more than most, but who our benefactor is, or in our case, who our guardian angel is, we have no idea."

"You now have to leave. God bless you for bringing me Don's diary. I feel he now knows the truth and we'll be together again sometime, somewhere. Under no circumstance come back here after you leave, or try to contact me again. It is much too dangerous and will put too many lives at risk. Antonio will show you the way out the back door. Goodbye and "Vaya con Dios." (Go with God)

She knocked on the wall and immediately the bartender came in, looked at her, nodded, and motioned me to follow him.

The next day, without any incident, I joined the scuba group flying back to the Caymans.

Flying to the Caymans and then back to Maine, I couldn't put this beautiful love story out of my head or the sacrifice one person can make for another. Maybe there's still hope for the human race. Maybe I should write this story.

EPILOGUE

*T*here's a beautiful hacienda in Matanzas, owned by the Cuban Government with a magnificent view of the Straits of Florida that, at one time, was owned and the home of generations of the Rodriguez family. A hacienda that was once surrounded by hundreds upon hundreds of acres of cane sugar and tobacco.

In it lives a world-renowned female pediatrician, her Aunt, a tired old man and the Doctor's young son.

Sometimes the old man tells stories of yesteryear to his grandson, tells stories of what used to be and how it was..

When his daughter is home, when the house is still, when all are asleep, he sits alone on the patio and after a few rums, watches the moon slowly drift across the night sky, turning the Straits of Florida to pale yellow. He reflects upon a time gone by, when his son had a friend that became a member of their family; his grandson's American father.

EPILOGO

*H*ay una hermosa hacienda en Matanzas, propiedad del Gobierno cubano con una magnífica vista sobre el estrecho de Florida, que pertenecía al mismo tiempo y en el hogar de las generaciones de la familia de Rodríguez. Una hacienda que una vez fue rodeada por cientos de cientos de hectáreas de cana de azúcar y tabaco.

En vive un renombre mundial femenino pedíatra, su tía, un anciano cansado y hijo del médico.

A veces el viejo narra historias de antaño a su nieto. Narra historias de lo que solía ser y cómo fue.

Cuando su hija es casa, cuando la casa está todavía, cuando todos están dormidos, se sienta sola en el patio y después unos rones, mira la Luna deriva lentamente en el cielo nocturno, pasando el estrecho de Florida a amarillo palido. Reflexionando sobre tiempo pasado cuando su hijo tenía un amigo que se convirtió en un miembro de su familia. Padre estadounidense de su nieto.